# DOUBLE ACT

Returning from several months spent filming her lead role in a brand new TV detective series, Phyllida Moon has misgivings about how she will be received at the Peter Piper Detective Agency. But she needn't worry – she's welcomed back with open arms. Also, Peter has just the job lined up for her...

Phyllida's new role is Sonia Sheridan, amateur actress extraordinaire, the job to expose the drug dealing thought to be taking place within the Little Theatre Company. Then one of the theatre company is murdered – and it looks like the killer could only be a fellow member...

# DOUBLE ACT

*by*

Eileen Dewhurst

**Magna Large Print Books**
Long Preston, North Yorkshire,
BD23 4ND, England.

British Library Cataloguing in Publication Data.

Dewhurst, Eileen
    Double act.

A catalogue record of this book is
available from the British Library

ISBN    0-7505-1601-1

First published in Great Britain 2000
by Severn House Publishers Ltd.

Published in Large Print 2001 by arrangement with
Severn House Publishers Ltd.

Magna Large Print is an imprint of Library Magna Books Ltd.

Printed and bound in Great Britain by
T.J. (International) Ltd., Cornwall, PL28 8RW

# One

During the party to celebrate the end of the filming of *A Policeman's Lot,* Phyllida Moon telephoned her boss in Seaminster to tell him she would be back at work in the Peter Piper Detective Agency the following Monday.

'That's great!'

'Thank you, Peter.' But had he hesitated?

'That's if you really want to come.' Behind her voice there was a great deal of cheerful noise, and he had a vague, uneasy picture of beautiful people and an irresistible life-style.

'Of course I do.'

'See you Monday, then. If that won't be too soon for you.'

'It won't. See you Monday.'

Phyllida tucked her mobile away with her uncharacteristic sense of triumph a little dented. She had rung Peter in the glow of it, to share her relief that in spite of the fun and the challenge and the excitement of filming a major TV series she was raring to get back to her other job.

But was he raring to reinstate her?

They would both be wary, Phyllida tried to tell herself as she slipped back into the party. She, because Peter might have found during her two-month absence that he could manage well enough without a second field assistant whose only special attribute was sleuthing in character. And Peter – if he really did want her back – because the member of his staff whose place he had kept open had just spent a couple of months filming a leading role in a prestigious new TV series and might have developed an exclusive taste for it.

'Ready for Seaminster, Phyllida?'

It was Patrick Varley, her producer and the only member of the *Policeman's Lot* team who knew she had a second career. And, true still to his promise to keep her secret, his query was a murmur into her ear.

'Yes. Does that surprise you?'

'Not knowing Phyllida Moon.'

'I hope Phyllida Moon can keep her anonymity, Patrick.'

'What a strange creature you are.'

'My other job—'

'I half believe you'd be happier anonymous even if you didn't have another job. But not to worry, when the credits roll the name Phyllida Moon won't be in them. And although in *A Policeman's Lot* you're not disguised, well...' Patrick studied her thoughtfully. 'You're so entirely different from what you are as yourself you'll probably get away with not being recognised.'

'I hope so; in Seaminster my anonymity's my disguise. I'm terrified of losing it.'

'I don't suppose you will. But make the most of the summer, dear, just in case.'

'Oh, I intend to. I'm off in the morning.'

The flat they had found her near the studio was cosy and comfortable, but Phyllida felt no pang as she packed up, even when the actor who had played office manager of the detective agency her character owned telephoned to ask her to stay on at least one more day so that they could meet *à deux*. She had grown fond of Ralph Harding over the hothouse weeks of shared stresses and panics, but only as she had grown fond of them all. Her heart, if she had one – Phyllida sometimes wondered, since in the end she had so easily let her errant husband go – had remained in Seaminster, the first place since her childhood where she had come to feel she belonged. She had to hope, of course, that *A Policeman's Lot* would run to a second series, but for the moment she was profoundly content to be going home.

She'd been back to her house a few times during the filming and it didn't feel stale or neglected, but immediately she arrived she went through it, opening windows. She then left it again and walked down the short stretch of sloping roadway to the promenade, where she crossed the road and then the wide seaward pavement of the Parade to lean her arms on the hyacinth-blue railings and draw a deep breath of contentment.

It was a warm June day but the railings were its brightest colour: the sluggish water was dove-grey under a pastel sun that was diffusing its warmth through a thin layer of cloud. The horizon was mist, yet light seemed to sparkle in the air around her, reflecting the lightness of her spirits. The filming had been a magnificent dream and she wanted it to recur, but it was wonderful to be home by the sea and about to resume her second career.

If Peter really did want her back.

As her spirits clouded Phyllida deplored the diffidence she seemed able to overcome only when she turned herself into another woman. Through her pleasure at being back by the sea – she was able, when she woke during the night, to tweak her curtain and see the dark heave of it – there ran a thread of anxiety that Peter the kind, the polite, might find it hard to bring himself to tell her he had found he could manage perfectly well without her.

By the morning a wind had sprung up, boisterous but mild and blowing from the west, so that Phyllida, reaching the promenade, fancied it chivvying her into town and back into what she realised, as it urged her along, she had come to think of as her normal life.

But it could only be that if Peter had come to think of it as normal, too.

While Phyllida was being blown along The Parade, Peter was marshalling the two-thirds of his team he had invited to come in that morning slightly earlier than usual.

'She's so polite and so kind,' he said to them, 'she may be feeling she owes it to us to come back. I want you two to observe her carefully, and tell me honestly if you think she's going through the motions.'

'A leading character in a TV crime series...' Steve spoke feelingly, slurping the words as if they were a mouthful of ice-cream. 'She doesn't need to look at us again.'

'But she will!' Jenny rounded on him indignantly, her spread of dark curls shaking with emotion and her face flooding pink. 'She *loves* working here! You shouldn't judge people by your own reactions, Steve!'

Steve shrugged, but his pale, sharp features coloured too at Jenny's rebuke. 'I want her to come back,' he admitted reluctantly. 'I'm only saying ... what if she's been offered another contract?'

'That's a possibility,' Peter conceded, with a pang that took him to his feet and over to the nearer of the two sash windows which were his personal share of the elegant façade behind which his agency practised on the second floor of the early Victorian building that formed one side of Dawlish Square. Jenny had another original front window in the outer office where she presided, but the general office, rest room, kitchen and bathroom were at the back and looked out on to the mirror image of another less than elegant Victorian rear, veined with drain-pipes. There were, however, two small gardens between the two buildings, walled and paved and carpeted in the spring with white pear blossom.

Dawlish Square was undisturbed Italian-ate stucco on its four sides round a formal garden as barbered as the back gardens were overgrown. Opposite the offices of the Peter Piper Agency was Seaminster's oldest hotel, the Golden Lion, where Phyllida had a permanent back room into which her characters – who always stayed at the hotel – disappeared and from which she emerged as her anonymous self to go home without fear of recognition by client or subject of investigation.

He had stood at that window, watching her coming or going, so many times that he wondered for a moment whether his sight of her now on one of the square's neat paths was an inward vision.

'She's here,' he said, going back to his chair. 'Don't forget what we've agreed to say. Has the kettle boiled?'

They were all in the outer office as the door opened, Jenny with Phyllida's mug in her hand, which she transferred the moment Phyllida had swung her bag off her shoulder.

They said, 'Welcome home!' in unison, and Phyllida said, 'Yes, I am home!' and all embarrassment was banished before it had time to take hold. It didn't threaten again until they were sitting round Peter's desk catching up, and Steve told Phyllida he'd

11

been half afraid they wouldn't see her again.

'Thanks for saying "afraid", Steve. But d'you really think my head would turn so easily?'

'If you were offered another good contract,' Steve mumbled, looking down at his knees to avoid Peter and Jenny's disapproving eyes.

'I wasn't, and I didn't want to be. Not yet, anyway. And another contract would only be for a limited time, like the one that's just expired. This is my long-term occupation.' As Peter's face lit up, Phyllida knew that if she worried again about her future with his agency she would have to accept that she was the victim of an anxiety neurosis. 'So, it's good to see you all. Have you got anything to suit me?'

Phyllida had learned to interpret the wary look that took over Peter's face: it meant he believed that he had, but suspected she might not like it.

'Peter?'

'Well... Quite an interesting situation, really...' Peter turned on Steve, then on Jenny, the mildly dismissive look they too had learned to interpret, and both got to their feet, Steve with a deep sigh of reluctance.

Phyllida murmured a sop as they left the room: they would talk more later. 'So?' she encouraged, the moment the door had closed. The adrenalin was flowing as strongly as it had flowed before the cameras.

'You're ready?' He had hoped for a little more time. 'If you want to talk a bit first about what you've been doing. Professionally,' he added quickly, rolling his eyes and tossing back the flop of fair hair on his brow. Phyllida reflected that they grew more like brother and sister by the day.

'Of course I do. But after I've heard about this job you're not sure I'm going to like.'

'How did you – oh, of course, I'd forgotten you're a witch. The thing is – funny thing, really, considering what you've just been doing – it would involve... Well, I'll tell you from the beginning.'

'Good.'

From her chair Phyllida could see over the low variegated rooftops to the sea. The wind was whipping it into white wavelets that looked like tiny moving rifts in a surface which as she watched warmed from pale grey to pale gold in a sudden flood of sunshine. Eager as she was to hear Peter's story, she found it an effort to turn her gaze back to him.

13

'I get that feeling about the sea too,' he said, 'when I've been away.'

A sister could not have had a more satisfactory younger brother. Phyllida always saw Peter as younger than she was although she was senior by only a couple of years. She had decided early on that it was his enthusiastically boyish air and the lean, loose-limbed body which from across the street made him look like a sixth-former rather than a man in his mid-thirties. In her mind he was her Peter Pan, although she seldom fell into the trap others sometimes occupied of underestimating his adult abilities.

'It's a sort of relief to be back beside it.'

'I know. Now.' He drew a deep breath. 'We've been approached by John Harper of Page and Harper, the Moss Street accountants, because he's worried that his son may be into drugs. Staying in his room alone or else going out and reluctant to say where, being secretive, not spending time in the family circle, that kind of thing. Harper hasn't noticed any physical changes, or been able to find anything tell-tale in the boy's room, but he's hardly eating, he's lost weight and he looks–' Peter glanced down at the paper in front of him – '"permanently done in" was the phrase Harper used. I asked him if his son's life had altered in any way they could put a name to, and he told me he thought the changes had begun when he joined a...' Peter hesitated, his expression the familiar mingling of entreaty and defiance which told Phyllida he was reaching the point in his story where he could no longer conceal its possible lack of appeal for her. 'An amateur dramatic society,' he brought out firmly, and went quickly on. 'He made a new friend, Ben Carson, who was already a member of the society and who the father thinks may have persuaded his son to join – he isn't sure which came first, the friendship or the interest in the society. Anyway, the change in the boy's behaviour started after he joined the society and made this new friend, a lad a few years older than himself – Paul Harper's eighteen and still at school. Bright, I read between the father's modest lines, and hoping for Oxford. His friend's twenty-two and works in an art gallery. The possible point is, a young chap arrested recently for heroin dealing – there was a lot in the local paper, but you were away – was a member of the society. The police don't seem to have made any connection between it and him,

15

but the society functions as a social club as well, and the dealer was still at large when Paul Harper joined it. The fact that his father can't see any physical signs of addiction makes him afraid Paul might be dealing rather than using, which frightens him just as much, obviously, in a different way.

'Now...' Peter leaned forward, his brown eyes pleading. 'The society is of course trying to distance itself from the scandal and is doing it positively by holding open auditions to attract new members. Knowing – hoping – you were about to come back, I told Harper I might be able to supply a would-be recruit–'

The last thing Phyllida had expected at that moment was a whoop of laughter, but Peter was suddenly falling back in his chair, gasping.

'I hadn't realised,' he managed in a moment, wiping his eyes, 'how bloody funny it is. You just coming from the top of the tree, and being immediately invited to grub around at the bottom. I'm sorry, Phyllida.'

'Don't be. I like it.'

Peter jerked upright in amazement. 'You do?'

'Yes. It'll be a marvellous way to watch all the suspects, like being part of a live Agatha Christie.'

'But the acting side. Maybe having some school mistress or office PA telling you how it should be done.'

'Which will amuse me immensely. And I've always got my get-out, Peter. Whoever I am can go into the Golden Lion one day and never come out again if it gets too much for me. But I doubt it will.'

'You're pure gold, as I've told you many times already. What sort of character d'you feel you should be?'

'Can I think about it? Can I, in fact, think about it till tomorrow morning?' Other thoughts – centred on a garden just outside town – were becoming insistent. 'You can contact your Mr Harper in the mean time and tell him you're able to provide a recruit.'

'Of course. Oh, Phyllida, that's wonderful! I know it could easily turn out to be a wild-goose chase, but if it isn't–'

'Chief Superintendent Kendrick will be reluctantly grateful yet again, and that bit more wary of Mary Bowden.' So far as the Agency was concerned, Phyllida's name appeared only on its private books. Mary

17

Bowden had had to be invented in a hurry the first time a couple of Phyllida's characters had helped the Chief Superintendent to the solving of a murder case; hers was the name under which Kendrick had questioned a charlady, a sophisticated American, and an elderly spinster, and both Phyllida and Peter were aware that he was not entirely convinced by Peter's assurance that the Agency employed only one female field operative. 'I wonder if he'll watch *A Policeman's Lot?*'

'I doubt it; a fictional police force is one thing he doesn't need.'

'But if he comes in while his wife's watching–'

'He's never knowingly seen *you*, Phyllida, and your TV character's hardly likely to remind him of any of the others he's met.'

'You're right. Anyway, I'm discovery-proof until the autumn, and then I'll have to hope I'm as unlike my TV character as my producer thinks I am. May I have the afternoon off, Peter? I'll be back to full-time work in the morning.'

'Of course. I was expecting you to take longer.'

'I don't need longer. I'll come in with some ideas about my character for the amateur dramatics.'

Steve had gone sleuthing and Jenny was regretfully too busy for a chat, so Phyllida went food shopping and then spent an hour happily gardening and thinking with only the odd flutter of trepidation about the rest of the day. At twelve noon, she drove out to Seaminster's small Botanic Gardens, a mile and a half inland from town.

She had met its director at an art class she had joined in character on her last assignment before filming, and he had been attracted by the red-haired, wry-minded Scotswoman recuperating at the Golden Lion. This was an occupational hazard with which she was familiar, as she was familiar with the bleak necessity of rejecting an overture she herself would have been interested in following up. Until now, this had been made easier by her painful knowledge that it was not Phyllida Moon her subject was interested in and that there was no real potential rapport. But the woman who had found favour with Dr Jack Pusey had been close enough to Phyllida's inward self, if not her outer, to give her the courage, when the case was over, to visit his Gardens in the hope of an encounter which might tell her whether there was a chance

19

that what had attracted him had been more than her disguise.

As she drove for the second time towards Jack Pusey's working domain, Phyllida recovered the sense of amazement she had felt the first time she had travelled that road, at finding herself unhesitating over an enterprise so wildly out of character. Something was compelling her, even while she continued to rejoice in the glorious sense of independence that had come with her decision to leave her husband; perhaps after all she did still have a heart.

On her first visit she had walked about the Gardens, enjoying their constantly changing character both in itself and as a reflection of the man in charge of them, and had ended up in the restaurant in the early afternoon on a memory of having sometimes seen senior members of a theatre company's management eating late in the theatre's restaurant.

And he had been there, broaching a hearty meal, and she had bought a coffee and a sandwich and sat down in his line of vision. They had smiled a couple of times when their eyes had met, and the photograph of him on the wall had enabled her to pause by his table as she went out and tell him how happy she felt in his Gardens. He had been pleased, he had thanked her formally, and then there had been the briefest of brief moments which was the reason she was going again: she had seen in his eyes what she had seen when he had looked at the red-haired Scotswoman.

Two months had dramatically altered the appearance of the Gardens, if not – to her renewed surprise – her sensations at being back there. The wind of the morning had died, but the brilliance that had accompanied it was persisting under a blue sky lightly whipped by cirrus. From one long vista, slowly rising, small themed gardens opened up on either side, even the most experimental laid out with regard for its appearance. Phyllida hardly expected to meet Dr Pusey in one of the small enclosed spaces, although she held her breath each time she entered one. In the event, on a Monday morning, she met scarcely anyone except for gardeners and working students of horticulture whom she stopped to compliment, and at a quarter to two, after several contemplative pauses on seats backed by old walls or high hedges, she made her way to the small restaurant.

There were a few people still eating, but

not the Gardens' director. Sitting down with her sandwich and coffee, Phyllida gave a wry inward smile at her sense of disappointment, considering it absurd even as she acknowledged it.

When she left the restaurant she went into the shop, bought some postcards of the Gardens through the seasons and decided it was time to get back on to her own patch of earth. As she reluctantly crossed the entrance hall she saw a notice-board and stopped to read it, smiling again at the quickening of her pulse as she discovered that the Sunday to come would be an Open Day on which members of staff would be available in the Gardens – or in the lecture theatre if wet – to answer visitors' queries. The Director would be present to open the proceedings at ten o'clock, and all were welcome...

Phyllida went to the outdoor plant shop and bought half a dozen house plants to celebrate her return home.

# Two

One of the things Phyllida had rediscovered since returning to live by the sea was its leading role in the drama of the weather. On the streets of London, the next morning would have been marked climatically by no more than blown litter and wet pavements, but in Seaminster the wind was dashing the tide against the sea wall and breaking it into spray which sparked over the blue railings to swell the rain lashing any pedestrians hardy enough to be staggering from blue lamp post to blue lamp post. Phyllida's concession to the battle of air and water was to walk close to the buildings on the townward side of the Parade and keep her head down. She could, of course, have gone to work by car – as she always arrived at and left the Golden Lion as herself, she could at all times park safely behind the hotel – but she had a lot of fresh air and exercise deprivation to make up for and, as yet, no trappings of another persona to carry with her to her working bedroom.

Peter was in the outer office when she arrived, and told her approvingly that she had some colour in her face.

'That has to be an achievement.' Phyllida had never seen colour in her sallow cheeks, but she could feel them glowing.

*'You walked!'* Jenny found it hard to believe that a woman with a car at her disposal should choose to expose herself to the morning's savagery. But then, Phyllida Moon appeared to have no personal vanity. Jenny could never quite decide whether to envy or to disapprove of the skimpy way Phyllida invariably made good any dishevelment by no more than a shake of her cap of what Jenny had to concede was well-cut hair. She was doing it now, and Jenny also had to concede that if you looked beyond the low-key impact you saw quality, even elegance, in Phyllida Moon's own unshowy self. And she was so *nice*. Jenny knew that her TV stardom wouldn't change her.

Peter was looking from one warily expectant youngster to the other. 'Leave the door open,' he said eventually, 'and both come in, it's time you knew about Phyllida's Next Case.' Phyllida heard the capital letters on a renewed surge of adrenalin as Jenny and Steve followed her into Peter's office, where she took her usual place in front of his desk. Jenny perched on a peripheral chair, and after an attempt to lean nonchalantly against the side of the desk, Steve reluctantly did the same.

'The chief suspect,' Peter began, starting to pace between the desk and his nearer window, 'is the Little Theatre Company, Seaminster's amateur dramatic society.'

Phyllida spent her second hearing of John Harper's brief wondering why it was making Jenny look so troubled, and whether she dare ask her.

'What we've got to decide now,' Peter finished, sitting down, 'is who Phyllida is going to send to the auditions.' Neither he nor Steve seemed aware of Jenny's dismay. 'If Phyllida hasn't decided already. I expect she has.'

'Subject to what you feel, Peter, I thought ... the maturely sophisticated American?' Phyllida was watching Steve.

'Wow!' Steve reddened and blinked, pressing his hands between his knees.

'You *are* silly,' Jenny told him.

'It's a tribute to Phyllida's talents,' Peter said, with swift tact. 'But she *is* rather old for you, Steve.'

'I like older women,' Steve protested. 'And

25

I met her before I met Phyllida.' When Phyllida had been signed to play her private eye role in *A Policeman's Lot* she had picked the Peter Piper Agency out of the local Yellow Pages and asked Peter for a job to gain hands-on experience for the part. He had politely declined to give her one so she had posed as a client, the husky-voiced American sophisticate whom Steve had fallen romantically in love with the moment she entered the office. 'She was a real person to me then,' he continued, his sharp cockney voice softening to wistfulness. 'And she still is. She was real to you both, too,' he went on, accusingly. 'That's why she got the job. At least I'm loyal!'

'Loyal? You!'

They all knew Jenny was thinking about Steve's long-suffering girlfriend Melanie, so adoring she accepted being picked up and set down to suit Steve's disordered private life, but it was unusual for her to reprimand him so sharply.

'Out of bed the wrong side this morning?' Steve inquired.

'All right, all right, you two! EGM closed and ad hoc sub-committee appointed. It will report in due course.' Peter nodded towards the door, and the two flushed juniors filed reluctantly out, closing it behind them.

'Something about this has got to Jenny,' Peter said, the moment the latch had clicked. 'See if you can find out what.'

'I noticed. Yes, I will.' Not for the first time, she had underestimated what she knew to be her boss's considerable powers of dissimulation. 'Do you think the American woman's right, Peter? Amateur societies tend to be short on glamour and the character's so distinctive she's unlikely to be asked to be anything much different from her apparent self. That should go for her appearance as well, so there won't be a need for disguise on disguise.'

'I can't see the charade getting as far as a dress rehearsal, but I agree your sophisticated American is the one, and it's not a bad idea to have someone from far enough away for you not to have to worry too much that her invented biographical details may be rumbled. And it could be that an obvious woman of the world, well enough heeled to live in a four-star hotel, might attract the attention of any drug-dealing member of the society. I think Harper said the first of the auditions is towards the end of the week, but I'll find out for sure when I give him the

27

good news. Now, d'you think you might whizz Jenny out for an early pizza?'

Phyllida offered the invitation tentatively, but Jenny jumped at it. 'That'd be great! I'd like to talk to you.'

'I hoped you would.'

Jenny stared. 'But you don't... Oh, of course, you were watching me when Peter–'

'So was he. Switch the phone through to him at twelve. He's expecting it.'

The outer door was opening, and Phyllida slid into the rest room. She appeared before clients only in disguise, and, if taken by one unawares, assumed the role of client herself. Peter found her half an hour later, reading one of the manuals on private investigative practice he had hopefully slipped in among the dog-eared thrillers and romances on the bookshelf.

'I've spoken to Harper, and he's over the moon. The auditions are on Thursday evening. Seven thirty at the Little Theatre. What are you going to call your American?'

'Sonia Sheridan keeps recurring.'

Peter considered. 'It has a nice ring to it; give it to Reception at the Golden Lion. Where does she hail from?'

'Texas. A little town not far from Houston, very like the little town featured in a Sunday supplement I forgot to throw away before I went to London. Two Oaks?'

'Fine. How did Jenny react to the idea of a lunch date?'

'Happily. She wants to talk to me so it doesn't look as if I'll have to do any probing. Unless knowing you noticed her reaction as well makes her a bit diffident – I have a feeling her emotions could be involved in some way. I'll tell her you're only interested in facts.'

'The fact of having you back here is fantastic,' Peter said fervently. 'What are you going to do now?'

'I thought I'd go over to the Golden Lion and make Sonia Sheridan's booking. And ask them to see that my bed's ready for Thursday night. If your office light's on when I get back from the theatre I may decide it's not worth going home after we've talked and I've shed Mrs Sheridan.'

Phyllida and Peter had never questioned one another about their home lives, but soon after she joined the Agency he had separated from a live-in girlfriend and started to spend a lot of time in the office – which, with its magnificent Victorian bathroom, modern Jenny-designed kitchen and becouched rest room, was an agreeable enough home from home. Although he had never formally invited Phyllida to join him there when she got back to the hotel after an evening's business, it had become an understanding between them that if his office light was on she would call in. Both of them found late-night chats useful, and Phyllida was glad of the opportunity to sort out her impressions of clients and situations aloud while they were still vivid.

When they saw her, the faces of both girls behind the Reception counter of the Golden Lion lit up. And then, to her relieved approval, went simultaneously deadpan as they awaited her approach. But they, and every other member of staff with whom Phyllida might come in contact, had been well schooled by their boss John Bright, who saw his debt to Peter for past services rendered as one he could never adequately repay.

'Good-morning,' they said in chorus, with the impersonal, querying inflexion they used to strangers.

'Good-morning. Linda. Sharon.' There was no one else within earshot. 'I'm back at work from today, and on Thursday a Mrs Sonia Sheridan will be arriving. American. Mature. You're met her type before. I expect she'll be in the foyer bar for a drink at about six thirty that evening.'

'We'll look forward to seeing her,' Sharon said.

'I don't expect to be sleeping here before Thursday night, and maybe not then, but I suggest you have the bed ready. I can never be sure I shan't need it.'

'Consider it done,' Wendy assured her. 'I hope you're feeling really better.'

John Bright's team had been told that Phyllida had spent the last couple of months having the operation for appendicitis she had in fact had three years earlier.

'Thanks. I'm fine.'

Dawlish Square was protected by the Golden Lion from winds blowing off the sea, but when Phyllida and Jenny turned into the narrow lane that led off it towards Moss Street and had no seaward buildings, it caught them with a triumphant squeal and they clung together, staggering towards the comparative shelter of shops and restaurants.

'We might get a corner table in Mario's,' Jenny gasped, as they warily separated and found they could walk upright. 'Flaming July!'

'Good idea. And we're almost there.'

The long, gloomy interior of the popular pizza café was as yet thinly sprinkled with customers, and two of the distant corner tables were unoccupied. 'Give me your order and bag one of the corners,' Jenny said. 'Peter's paying.' She hesitated. 'Did you tell him in so many words that I'd asked for a chat?'

'Yes. But I told you he saw for himself that something was wrong.' Phyllida's anxiety vanished as she realized Jenny was looking pleased.

'Isn't he amazing? I was convinced he hadn't noticed anything. When he told me to take the money out of the petty cash he just said he'd heard you and I were having lunch and let it be on the house. What are you having?'

Phyllida was glad to see that Jenny's appetite was unaffected by whatever was worrying her, and let her take the edge off it before suggesting she start to talk.

Jenny put her knife and fork back on her plate for the first time since she had begun to tackle her by now half eaten pizza. 'I think I'd have to tell you,' she said. 'Even if I didn't want to. Because of it perhaps being useful. But I do want to, because I want some advice, and I can't ask anyone at home.'

'I thought you could talk to your mother.' Phyllida put her knife and fork together beside her own unfinished pizza, defeated.

'I can, usually. But not over this, because I know she'd tell me to finish with Kevin. To be on the safe side.'

Phyllida thought she had just heard a quote. 'I think you'd better begin at the beginning.'

Jenny picked up her fork, and looked down at the food she began to toy with as she spoke. 'There's hardly anything to say. About three months ago I started going out with a chap called Kevin Keithley. I like him – a lot.' Colour flooded Jenny's face, and she paused to cut and swallow another mouthful. 'Phyllida,' she said through it, her eyes still down, 'he's a member of the Little Theatre Company, and he knew Hugh Barnes, the chap who got picked up for drug dealing. He made a great show of being shocked and surprised, but I was worried a bit even then, and now... You see, he knows the Harper boy. We went out in a foursome a couple of months ago.' Jenny raised pleading eyes to Phyllida, pushing her plate away.

'Thank you, Jenny,' Phyllida said carefully. 'Yes, this could be useful. How did the Harper boy seem?'

Jenny shrugged. 'OK. Not the way Peter described him.'

'Was this before Barnes was picked up?'

'Yes.'

'You knew Barnes? You met him through Kevin?'

'No! I never met him; he was arrested before I ever went to the Little Theatre. And Kevin told me he didn't know him either, except as a fellow member of the Company. It's only now,' Jenny went on miserably, 'now that Peter's told us that maybe another two chaps are involved ... Phyllida, I'm really gone on Kevin, but if you think ... D'you think I should stop seeing him?'

'No!' Phyllida hoped the strength of her reaction was as much to do with Jenny's feelings as with the help the girl might be to the Agency if she continued with the relationship. 'There's no need, Jenny,' she went on more gently. 'You've no proof at all that he was involved in any way with the boy who was picked up, or with Paul Harper. What does he do? Your Kevin?'

'He's awfully clever,' Jenny said proudly. 'He read Maths at university – Bristol – and he's started training to be an accountant. I can't think what he sees in me.'

Phyllida had got to know Jenny well enough to believe her puzzled expression reflected a genuine amazement and not to be surprised that the promising student had been able to recognise the bright intelligence behind the girl's conventionally glamorous exterior. 'You're clever too, Jenny. The office would collapse without you. Don't under-estimate yourself. And try not to worry about Kevin. Go on enjoying your friendship unless and until you see or hear something that worries you, and then tell me or Peter. And there's another thing: Sonia Sheridan – that's the name Peter and I have decided on for my American widow – will be around if she passes her audition, and she'll have an eye out.'

'I feel dreadfully disloyal,' Jenny said, 'even suspecting Kevin might be involved.'

'But with this latest twist, you can't help it. We've got to remember, though, that the arrest could have made an end of the drugs connection, and Paul Harper may have something totally different on his mind. Peter's told me there's no evidence at the moment that the Company has any ongoing connection with drug dealing or drug taking. But I'll have to tell him what you've told me, you know that. Unless you'd rather tell him yourself?'

'I'd rather you tell him. Oh, Phyllida, thank you. I feel so much better. When you're brooding on something on your own... There were some really gooey éclairs under the counter. Would you like one?'

'No thanks, but you go ahead if you don't think it will be too unkind to that hour-glass figure of yours.' Jenny had a generous bosom, a tiny waist, and modestly rounded hips under her habitual short tight skirts, and the effect was pleasing, especially to the young men who tended to pause and stare when Jenny and Phyllida were out together.

Jenny sighed. 'I'll make it a black coffee. Two?'

Phyllida nodded. 'Then you can tell me all about how you and Kevin met.'

Peter had indicated before she went out that he would be at her disposal when she returned for briefing about Jenny's revelations, and by the time they cringed back into the wind Phyllida had a fair-sized mental dossier on Jenny's latest boyfriend.

But Peter met her in his office doorway, a slip of paper in his hand. 'Harper senior has shown his gratitude in advance with a ticket

36

for this afternoon's matinee.' He ushered her inside as Jenny attacked the switchboard. 'He offered two, but I told him one would suffice. You've got just over an hour to decide whether to go as Phyllida Moon, or one of those fade-into-the-background market researcher types you're so good at. Actually, I don't see why you can't do this as yourself – a resting actress writing a book about the history of women and the stage. And I can imagine Phyllida Moon being pretty good at steering clear of conversations if she'd rather not get into them.'

'She is.' It was silly to feel alarmed at the prospect of being on a job as herself, but it had made her remember a dream she had had recently, in which she had been naked in a bedroom bounded by iron bars in place of walls. 'You're right. I'll go as myself. I didn't realise the society had a current production.'

'You haven't been back long enough to notice the posters.' Fleetingly Peter wondered where Phyllida had been the previous afternoon, and what she had been doing. It didn't look as if she had been in town, where there seemed to be a defiant poster, proclaiming business as usual, in every other shop window.

'I might have noticed one just now, only the wind made us keep our heads down.' Phyllida looked at the ticket. *'Death Comes Smiling.* Does that mean a murder mystery? Do you know?'

'All Harper told me was that the play was written by a top member of the Company whose name I can't remember. And that he produces his own and other plays, and appears in his own in a cameo role he always writes in for himself, à la Hitchcock.'

'Delusions of grandeur?'

'You'll find out.'

'Yes.' The adrenalin was flowing. 'Will you be here later? I've things to report on my conversation with Jenny.'

'Of course. But make it after six, when she'll have gone.'

Phyllida had been inside the Little Theatre – venue for amateur societies from other, smaller, conurbations inland and along the coast as well as for Seaminster's own company – just once, early in the Independent Theatre Company's repertory visit. She had gone with her husband – the company's stage manager – and his crony the producer to boost their egos. It was not a happy memory: Gerald and Wayne had sniggered their way through a production which Phyllida could have enjoyed and which she found worthy of respect, and after the interval, angry and ashamed, she had left them to it.

The Little Theatre was in Moss Street, a few façades beyond the pizza house where she and Jenny had lunched, and as she retraced her steps – more comfortably in the dying of the morning's dramatic wind – Phyllida reflected on the good fortune of the companies who played there. It had been purpose-built in the 1870s as a repertory theatre over what was then known as an emporium, and when that had closed in the twenties a local philanthropist with an interest in amateur theatre had bought it and handed it over to the theatre trustees for dressing rooms and props, freeing space upstairs for a patrons' coffee lounge, small rehearsal room and large green-room. The grand entrance to the emporium had been retained after several narrow escapes from would-be redevelopers, and patrons were faced on entry with a magnificent central staircase leading up to another, more modest but still elegant foyer off which opened the auditorium, the coffee lounge, and the Company's luxurious facilities. No doubt another more modest staircase led down behind the stage to the players' working domain on the ground floor: she would find out soon enough, if Sonia Sheridan made the impression Phyllida was confident of her making. Phyllida's confidence in her characters amused her in a rueful sort of way because of the contrast with her lack of confidence in her unadorned self.

A trickle of people was moving up the grand staircase and Phyllida joined it, recalling, rueful again, that even the professional Independent Theatre Company had been grateful for half-full houses at summer matinees. This was a poor day for July, though, and as a professional thespian with a feeling for her amateur fellows, she was glad to see as the lights were lowered that the over-sized auditorium contained at least as many clients as empty seats.

The play could have done as well as *The Mousetrap*, Phyllida had decided half-way through the first act, had it, too, made its debut in the nineteen-fifties. It was well-constructed and kind to its players, moving along at an admirably smooth and swift pace so that none of them was required to be spare for any length of time, the bane of the amateur thespian. But Phyllida found the language a slightly uncomfortable amalgam of the high-flown and the hearty, and at one point heard the urgent signature tune of *Dick Barton* playing somewhere at the back of her mind.

The first interval was a mere five minutes, but the second was billed to last twenty and she went with the flow into the coffee lounge where, cup and saucer in hand, she moved slowly along a repellent row of aggressive abstracts, ears at the ready. As so often in this kind of situation she was rewarded, just as the bell began ringing to summon the audience back to its seats.

'There he is. There's the author.' Slowly Phyllida half turned, to see a stout female elbow immediately behind her nudging a stout female side. Both women were staring at the bar, and Phyllida followed their gaze. It was easy to spot their target, a tall thin man leaning alone on the bar counter. 'He writes a lot of their plays, you know. Real dramas as well as whodunnits.'

That was it! Phyllida realised. That was what she had been aware of in his script without being able to define it. Henry Hutton – as the programme announced him – preferred to write serious plays, and *Death Comes Smiling* had been a potboiling

41

straitjacket. Observing him, she had to admit that he looked the serious dramatist's part – tall, lean, sharp-boned, with a fine head of grey-white hair crowning a brown parchment of a complexion and an expression of weary gravitas. Phyllida also suspected that he was aware of himself and the impression he hoped he was creating.

In the foyer, a large lady with white hair and a warm loud voice was telling a couple of female enquirers that yes, the first auditions were on Thursday of that week.

'Do come along,' she urged heartily. 'The more the merrier and we're always looking for talent, hidden or revealed.'

She ended with a loud laugh as her glance fell indifferently on Phyllida, where it lost its exuberance before she bustled busily away.

## Three

At a quarter to three the following afternoon, a red saloon car drew up alongside a stretch of pavement in one of the newer housing developments on the landward outskirts of Seaminster. After a few moments a man emerged, looked quickly up and down the curve of the road, and walked rapidly back the way he had just driven. When he had passed three houses he looked both ways again before walking more slowly, and with a show of nonchalance, up the short driveway to the front door of the fourth.

It was opened within seconds by a young woman in jeans and sweatshirt. The man was swiftly admitted and the door was closed.

Fifteen minutes later the door bell rang again. This time the young woman took longer to answer it, and when she did so she opened the door a grudging crack.

It was enough to show her second caller that she was now wearing a housecoat.

'Mrs Handley?' the caller inquired.

'There's no Mrs Handley living here,' the woman informed her coldly. 'You've got the wrong house.' She glanced behind her with a frown, towards a staircase.

'Oh, dear!' The woman on the doorstep was both flushed and flustered. 'This is my first call on a new job – market research, you know – and I seem to have made a mess of it! I was told–' She glanced down at the clipboard in her hand. 'Mrs Handley, 11 Crocus Close.' The clipboard fell from her hand on to the householder's bare foot.

'D'you mind?' The bare foot nudged it back over the threshold, and the caller bent clumsily to pick it up. Everything about her was clumsy, the householder noted distastefully: her hair had been hacked rather than cut, her nose was red as well as shiny, and her mackintosh – wildly inappropriate for such a nice warm day – was appalling. She wasn't going to last five minutes. 'I expect you want Crocus Place,' she said, the agreeable sensation of superiority making her momentarily generous. 'I can't think why they used two names so much alike so near together. I'm always getting–'

Both women heard the sound from the top of the stairs, and the one inside, after another swift backward look, started to close her front door. 'I'm sorry,' she said, 'you want Crocus Place.'

'D'you know Mrs Handley?' the caller pleaded.

'No. Sorry.' The door closed.

After a fumbling attempt to marshall the material in her hands the woman made her way back to the road, passed the red saloon, and got into a car parked a few yards beyond it. She sat writing for a few moments before driving away.

'If they were all as easy!' Phyllida said to

Peter an hour later, after a visit to the Golden Lion to shed the most pathetic in her range of characters. 'Not that I'd want them to be, but I quite like the neatness of this sort of assignment now and again.'

'So our client's fears are justified?'

'Absolutely. I saw the man go in – a superficially jaunty type, looked better to a naked eye than through a zoom lens – and he hadn't come out when I rang the bell. The subject had exchanged her day clothes for a housecoat, and kept glancing towards the staircase. I heard someone up there before she shut me out.'

'D'you think she suspected anything?'

'Not for a moment.'

'Not that it matters, we've got our evidence. Thanks.'

'Anything for tomorrow before I transform into Sonia Sheridan?'

Peter hesitated, the familiar look of wary entreaty suddenly in his eyes. 'You could be around here in the morning. I've got to be out on the Dolby case. So if Jenny were to ask her cousin if she could do another stint...'

'Her cousin would say yes.'

Jenny's non-existent cousin was currently on the dole, and glad of the odd hour's office sitting. She was as concerned with her appearance as Jenny was with hers, but the result was rather less discreet. In fact Jenny's cousin's appearance veered towards the tart whose identity Phyllida – to Peter's abiding amazement – could so convincingly assume. She had chosen Mandy as her office character because out of all those she had so far created the Mandy-type took the least time and effort to obliterate Phyllida Moon.

The long summer evening made it possible to garden herself into a tiredness where there was no room for any thoughts beyond bath and bed, but Phyllida reflected as she hauled her weary legs up the stairs that acting in the usual sense, even in front of TV cameras – learning a script and then playing it inside its defined parameters with everyone involved invulnerable to hurt in their awareness of the charade – was child's play beside the sort of role she was about to resume. Her sleep was restless, streaked with dreams which in the morning she recalled as a series of searches for a room which she knew was hers but which she never found.

Although the weather was restored to traditional summer, warm, sunny and windless, she had both Mandy and Sonia

Sheridan to take with her and decided to drive to her usual spot behind the Golden Lion. As usual, too, she took herself and her baggage in at the back door and up the back staircase – her room, in any case, was the rear side of the particular fire door that marked the change from high to low pile corridor carpet.

When she had disposed of her props Phyllida rang down.

'Miss Moon?'

'Just to prepare you, Linda. A young woman of the kind you're inclined to keep an eye on will be strolling through the foyer in twenty minutes or so. Lots of blonde hair, short tight black skirt, black choker with a phoney carnation. She won't linger. And when she comes back at lunchtime she'll go straight through to the back stairs.'

'Fine. I'll pass it on. The American lady?'

'She'll be around at about half-past six.' For a drink in the foyer bar before taking a taxi to the Little Theatre, to give Phyllida a chance to reacquaint them with each other in public. A post-prandial drink: she'd have an early supper, her mind always functioned better when her stomach was full. 'Could you ask Mario to send me up a slice of any sort of quiche and a salad at five? With a big pot of coffee?'

'Of course, Miss Moon.' The voice hesitated, then resumed in a non-conspiratorial rush. 'It's really good to have you back!'

'It's good to be back.'

Bringing Mandy into existence took just over half an hour. As always, Phyllida's mental processes kept pace with the changes she made to her appearance, and when she sat down in front of the dressing-table mirror for a final assessment of her transformation she saw that her mouth was slack and that she was flirting with her reflected face. She felt the stab of surprise that still struck her as she realised how much she had enjoyed turning into Mandy. Perhaps because the contrast between them was so liberatingly great.

Except when she was out on the street, having to parry both male warmth and female chill. In public at night – on Peter's orders and in accordance with her own sense of self-preservation – Phyllida always covered as much as she could of Mandy's flaunted availability with the long raincoat that hung permanently in her hotel wardrobe, and took taxis to and from her assignment. The Mandy who worked for the Peter Piper Agency could not, of course, in the interests of the Agency's reputation, be as blatantly available as Phyllida's professional prostitute, but even so Phyllida had to brace herself to cross Dawlish Square. This time she reached the sanctuary of the Agency building with no more than the audible tutting of an elderly woman and the slowing step of a young man who looked angry when he saw her own expression in Mandy's face.

Steve and Jenny were in the outer office, Steve lolling against a doorpost in a habitual pose and Jenny behind the reception counter. When Phyllida appeared there was a moment of hesitation in both faces, before Steve grinned and – as always when Mandy appeared – Jenny coloured. Phyllida was afraid it might be from embarrassment at having to claim this ambiguous female as her cousin.

'Peter's gone,' Jenny said, the rose leaving her pale skin as she studied Mandy. 'Phyllida, does it make you feel – well – different?'

'Not at this moment. But when I'm on stage – I mean, if a client came in now – I'd try to think myself into what I look like. Academic, I'm afraid, with this particular character.'

'Pity.' Steve left his prop and strolled up to Phyllida. 'Not that you're my type,' he murmured, studying her. Phyllida heard Jenny's sharp intake of breath, and offered herself a rare moment of self-congratulation: Steve would never have spoken so disrespectfully to Miss Moon.

'You'd better get going!' Jenny urged him. 'Peter told you the earlier the better.'

'All right, all right, I'm off.' Steve's irritation melted into entreaty as he turned back to Phyllida. 'The American... When will we see her?'

'Not today, Steve, I'll be going from the hotel to the theatre and the theatre to the hotel.'

'And that means she'll be going straight out when she comes downstairs, and straight up to bed when she gets back?'

'She may call on Peter before retiring. But that, as you know, is a strict twosome.'

'Before the theatre?'

Phyllida relented. 'She might have a drink in the foyer bar at half-past six or so. I've got to get used to her again.'

'There's no way she could know *you*, Steve!' Jenny admonished. 'Or consider getting to know you.'

'Give me some credit!' Steve countered

crossly. 'D'you think I'd ever put an operation at risk?'

'Of course not!' Phyllida swiftly intervened. 'I wouldn't have told you what I was planning if I thought for a moment you'd do anything to jeopardize my charade.' She hesitated. 'That's all Sonia Sheridan is, Steve. A charade.'

Steve marched to the door without another word, and Phyllida realised that the Mandy make-up was distorting the smile she had intended to soften her message. She put her hand on his arm as he passed her. 'I'm flattered,' she said. 'And I like the American woman, too.'

'Okay.' Steve grinned a truce before disappearing.

Jenny sighed audibly as the door closed. 'He's mad.' She turned a worried face to Phyllida. 'Is he really obsessed, d'you think?'

'I hope not. And it would be too utterly absurd; I have to believe he's down-to-earth enough to know that. I just think the American woman sums up for him what he sees as sophistication.' Phyllida saw for Steve a possibly painful contradiction between his reach and his grasp, and sometimes feared for him.

'At least he's not attracted by Mandy,'

Jenny conceded, then coloured again. 'Sorry, Phyllida!'

'For a compliment? I'll be in the inner office until you want me to take over Reception. Retire for your lunch whenever you want to.'

One of the two female would-be clients who came in while Jenny was in the rest room was so obviously unnerved by Mandy that Phyllida summoned Jenny to take over before the woman fled, regretfully deciding she must switch her office character to the fade-into-the-background market researcher type who was so much less fun and so much harder to impose on herself to the point of her complete obliteration.

She kept out of the way until Peter came back, then followed him into his office. She had intended asking him first how his morning had gone, but the instinctive recoil he hastened to replace with a smile made her tell him at once what was on her mind.

'I chose Mandy for the office,' she said. 'And now I'm choosing to replace her. Probably with the market researcher type. Mandy's not good for your image, Peter.'

'Well...' Now he was trying to replace his look of relief with a reflective frown. 'If you think so.'

'I know so. I chose Mandy because I put my self-preservation first. Because she's such a complete disguise and easy to put on. I think I've always felt she was wrong for the office, but I wouldn't face it. I'm sorry, Peter, she almost lost you a client this morning. And why in heaven's name didn't you say something?' she demanded, suddenly angry with his invariable politeness. 'You knew from the start she was wrong. Didn't you? Go on!'

Peter blinked and smiled. 'You do tone her down.'

'Peter! Please!'

'I'll be happier with the market researcher.' Peter paused, looking curious. 'Were you really putting yourself first? If you were I'm glad. I think one should sometimes, and I've always thought you never did. But, well, I did have my doubts about Mandy.'

'Thank you!'

'Jenny'll be pleased. She didn't really want her as a cousin.'

'I don't wonder. That was selfish, too. Now I'm going to get rid of her.'

'This market researcher,' Peter said musingly. 'Mary Bowden in one person at last? The Chief Superintendent would be happier talking to her as a single persona rather than a series of women he just can't accept are one and the same. And she's already an unofficial part of the establishment. I can't think why we haven't thought of this before. You'd be able to do far more than Mandy could, like interview would-be clients when I'm out and about, or here and tied up.'

'And a physical Mary Bowden would mean I'd always have a role in the office – if I'm not out on a case I'll be able to stay around without hiding.'

'D'you like the idea of interviewing?' Peter asked curiously.

'Yes. I didn't know I did until you suggested it, but I do. And the Mary Bowden character shouldn't be too hard to work out, or keep up.' Not too easy either, though, Phyllida hoped.

'So she'll be made flesh at last. But not this afternoon; you've got a big night ahead of you.'

Sometimes Phyllida went from one character to another without the intermediary of herself, but Mrs Sheridan was so dramatic a contrast to Mandy she needed a break between them. She toyed with the idea of

54

going home, but there would be too little time there for her to be able to forget the clock and she decided to lie on her hotel bed and sleep if sleep came, secure in her knowledge that her early supper would be her alarm clock. During her months at the Agency she had learned to make relaxed use of her time between characters, however short.

She was even able to think of Sunday's Open Day at the Botanical Gardens, and fall asleep on an image of the large kind presence of its Director. But when the knock came at her door and she had admitted a waiter with a tray, she thought of nothing but her imminent metamorphosis while she ate and drank, propped up in bed with the tray across her knees.

The character Phyllida was this time to call Sonia Sheridan was the only one of her characters, so far, who had made her aware of a sensation she had never experienced as herself: the confidence of knowing that wherever she went she was turning heads. Even on the stage, despite her assessment by a succession of producers as a good actress, she had rarely been given a glamorous role, and it had been dazzlingly exciting the first time she had assumed the American woman and experienced the effect of her on Peter and his staff. She had after that tentatively wondered if she might be able to annex some of the charisma for herself, but had wakened the next morning already deriding herself for the pathetic illusion and had set about getting her excitement under control by reminding herself, with severe regularity, that Phyllida Moon had no visible part in her character's impact. She had not, though, been entirely surprised by it: she had always suspected herself of the ability to transmit glamour through an assumed personality, but had lacked the confidence in her own which would have enabled her to ask a producer to give her a chance to show it.

There was plenty of time, and she took the transformation at a slow pace, inducing in herself as well as in Sonia Sheridan a sense of luxury. First she bathed, then anointed her tall, slim body with the lotion she associated with all her American sophisticate's manifestations, feeling it start to transform her as she gave her arms and legs their unaccustomed caresses.

When she came out of the bathroom wearing Sonia's cream satin underwear she moved across to the dressing-table with

Sonia's languid gait without instructing herself to do so, and smiled her acknowledgement of the reflex into Sonia's lazily amused eyes. When she had finished her make-up the eyes in the mirror were larger, the cheekbones more prominent and the mouth had an ironic twist. Mrs Sheridan, like a couple of her predecessors, was an ash blonde, and with the descent of the large-frame wig over her own close cap of hair Phyllida felt the invariable frisson that always flared through her in the moment her metamorphosis was complete – putting on the gold satin blouse and honey-coloured skirt and jacket were no more than flourishes to the completed work of art.

How would Dr Pusey react to Sonia Sheridan?

It was an idle thought, a superficial curiosity, which she dismissed as both unprofessional and academic the moment it came into her mind; she had no intention, now, of presenting the Director of Sea-minster's Botanical Gardens with anyone but Phyllida Moon.

It was Sonia Sheridan who told her off, aloud and good-naturedly, but when she had come down the elegant front staircase Phyllida went across to Reception to test the

American's husky voice in conversation.

'Everything satisfactory, madam?'

The sparkle in Linda's eyes confirmed Phyllida's hope that John Bright's young team enjoyed being part of the charade.

'Very satisfactory,' Mrs Sheridan drawled, looking at the small gold watch on her left wrist. 'Can you have a taxi here for me at seven?'

'Of course, madam.'

'Thanks. I'll be at the bar.'

Sonia Sheridan strolled across the foyer and settled herself on a bar stool. Mick, the chief barman, was polishing glasses, and turned with a welcoming smile to his elegant client. 'Yes, madam?'

Their eyes met, in fleeting complicity.

'A very dry Martini, please, with ice.' In a character like Sonia Sheridan, she could order her own favourite drink.

'And for you, sir?'

Mick had put an art deco cocktail glass in front of her, and was moving along the bar as he spoke. Through the mirror that ran the length of the counter Phyllida watched him reach the lone customer at its far end close to the hotel entrance. She couldn't hear the man give his order, but she watched with disguised interest as Mick served him, smiling to herself as a Scotch and soda were supplied.

Steve sat morosely staring into it, lifting his head only to look into the mirror. He appeared unaware of the attractive woman perched at the other end of the bar, and the gaze that intermittently met hers in the glass showed no sign of recognition.

Phyllida decided not to tick him off the next morning, not even to refer to his visit to the Golden Lion. But as she strolled past him to the door and Mrs Sheridan's taxi, she resisted her impulse to put a hand on his slumped shoulder.

## Four

This time the large lady with the white hair and big voice bustled towards Phyllida instead of away from her. She was waiting in the splendour of the downstairs foyer to encourage the small group of would-be thespians and stage staff who had tentatively converged on the art deco doors of the Little Theatre a couple of minutes short of seven thirty.

'Come in! Come in! You're all most welcome!' But it was Sonia Sheridan on whom her smiling gaze was fixed. 'I'm Amy Tate, co-Chair of the Little Theatre Company. We're about to cast a play, but we're also thinking beyond that to the longer future, so there's plenty of scope. Now, if you'd like to go through...'

A further contingent was entering the foyer, and Miss Tate reluctantly withdrew her gaze from Mrs Sheridan and began to repeat her words of welcome. Phyllida allowed the other members of her group to set the pace across the upstairs foyer to the swing doors at the back, then strolled in their wake. The tall thin man she had seen the day before at the patrons' bar was drooping beyond the green-room door and welcomed them in a soft, tired voice which was in such contrast to Miss Tate's enthusiasm that Phyllida looked forward to the entertainment of seeing them together.

'Come in, do. I'm Henry Hutton, writer, actor and producer.' Unlike Miss Tate, Mr Hutton evidently did not rate his co-Chairship high enough to include it in his oral CV. He waved a limp hand towards a door on the far side of a room attractively set with armchairs, sofas and small tables.

'Please go through into the rehearsal room and find yourselves seats.'

Beyond the far door was a non-upholstered space smaller than the first room, in which several rows of wooden chairs had been arranged in a semi-circle facing a low stage. For rehearsals of small scenes and weak spots, Phyllida decided; there was no way a full production could have been crowded in.

On the stage now were a short row of empty chairs and a few people standing about. As Phyllida's party appeared – the first members of the public to arrive – one of them, a slim, attractive young woman with long, shining blonde hair, came down the few shallow steps to meet them.

'Hello! I'm Carol Swain, secretary and dogsbody.' But the strong-featured, intelligent face suggested qualities of leadership. 'Glad to see you. If you'd like to sit down. Anywhere will do...'

Sonia Sheridan chose a chair at the near end of the second row, and Phyllida began her mental log of the few people who had been in the rehearsal room when the audition seekers entered. She looked first at the stage, and with a leap of the heart that set the adrenalin flowing she recognized her central subject, Paul Harper, from the photograph his father had supplied: tall, thin and fair, with eyes large and blue enough to show their colour across the distance he stood from her. Self-conscious, she quickly saw, despite the charming smile with which he responded to being spoken to. And, when not speaking, warily tense – Phyllida thought she would have noticed the tension even if she hadn't been studying him so closely. His appearance was in sharp contrast with the young man standing nearby: shorter, stockier, with a lot of wavy black hair, a swarthy complexion and dark, deep-set eyes. Ben Carson, the friend Harper senior mistrusted? The expression in the dark eyes was predominantly grave, to the point of sadness, it seemed to Phyllida, as he watched Carol Swain climb the few steps at the side of the stage. As she came up to the two men she slipped her hand into Carson's and they stood linked as the three of them talked. Probably his fiancée, mentioned in the file on young Harper.

'It could be rather amusing, I suppose.'

So Sonia Sheridan had reflected her own inward smile. On a shaft of alarm Phyllida turned towards the voice. It came from Henry Hutton, who appeared to have abandoned his reluctant role as joint host. His thin face, Phyllida was already aware, was one of those which are only slightly less unnerving than the faces that are always smiling: the faces that give nothing of their owners' reactions away.

'I'm sorry,' Mrs Sheridan drawled, smiling openly now so that Henry Hutton was forced to offer in return a fleeting stretch of the lips. 'I was thinking about something quite other. I'm sorry if I appeared rude.'

'My dear lady.' The disclaimer was elegantly given. 'I was just watching the proceedings – or lack of them – through another's eyes for a moment, and understanding what I thought was your reaction.' Henry Hutton paused, gravely regarding her. 'I hope you are here as a would-be actress rather than for stage management. We lack intelligent glamour.'

'Thank you. Yes, I am.' For an absurd moment, Phyllida was jealous of the woman she had created. 'And that was a very fine compliment.' All the more effective for there being no indication in Hutton's face of the impression Sonia Sheridan had made on him. 'But I *am* a tad worried about getting my tongue around your Queen's English.'

He shrugged. 'I expect you'll manage well

enough. I wrote the play we're putting on next and there's a part in it that can easily cross the Atlantic.'

'You must hear me read before you have any thoughts about that,' Sonia modestly advised. 'But I should love to act in something you've written – I saw your current production this week and was impressed. Very fast moving and professional.'

'Thank you.' The poker face was unable to entirely hide Henry Hutton's gratification, which appeared briefly in a warming of the cold grey eyes and a slight relaxation of the mouth. An attractive mouth, Phyllida idly conceded, the thin lips sharply but delicately defined.

'It gave me, though–'

'Yes?' Henry Hutton sat down in the chair in front of Phyllida's and turned round, encircling the chair top with his arms.

'The feeling that you were – well, doing a business job. That you wanted to be writing something with more feeling, substance.'

'You're very perceptive, Mrs–'

'Sheridan. Sonia Sheridan.'

'Mrs Sheridan. That is exactly what I do want. And hope I have achieved it to some extent in the new play, without losing the – how shall I put it? – the necessity, at an amateur box office, of not straying too far outside what the audience expects, and what the cast is comfortable with.'

'It sounds very intriguing.'

Henry Hutton again showed, fleetingly, his favourable reaction to Sonia's smile, although it was clear to Phyllida that he was approving it as he might approve a well-painted smile on a female portrait – there was no personal male reaction. 'I hope it won't disappoint you.'

'I'm sure not. Are we reading from it tonight?'

'No, no.' Henry Hutton's voice was pained and he gave a delicate little shudder, no doubt at the idea of his play being mauled in the mouths of the untalented. Phyllida was glad he had chosen to sit in front of her; it enabled her to continue an intermittent observation of the people on the stage. Now, following the settling in the audience of a third small group of arrivals, Miss Tate had puffed her way up on to the stage, where she was fussily attempting to allocate places. 'I thought – Miss Tate and I thought – some Shakespeare. Always so revealing, whether or not one of the plays is subsequently performed. We have in fact done a couple of the comedies... And then some Barrie. Dated in many ways, of course, but always popular with provincial audiences' – Henry Hutton used the phrase so naturally it was almost free of condescension – 'and undeniably well constructed, with good parts. I thought–'

'Henry!' Amy Tate called bracingly, and Phyllida saw that Harper, Carson, Carol Swain and a middle-aged man with red hair and glasses had been persuaded to sit down. Ben Carson was sitting between Carol and Paul Harper, and as he turned towards the girl his face lit up with an affectionate smile which for a brief moment dramatically lightened his grave expression. 'D'you think we might get started?' Amy Tate went on. 'If anyone else is coming they'll be late and will expect us to be under way.'

Phyllida heard the deep sigh as Henry Hutton turned round to face the stage.

'Of course, Amy, of course.' He got to his feet, retrieved a sheaf of papers from a table by the wall and slowly ascended the stage, where he and Miss Tate sat down side by side on the two remaining empty chairs.

For a few moments they consulted together, and then Miss Tate rose again and stood smiling upon her audience, which Phyllida reckoned without counting must now number about twenty-five.

'Welcome, all!' she announced, with loud enthusiasm, and as Henry Hutton seemed to shrink even farther into himself Phyllida fancied Miss Tate drawing on his small store of energy to swell her own natural ebullience. 'Now, before we start our proceedings tonight, I have a few words to say to you all as Chair – co-Chair – of the Company.' Henry Hutton's eyes briefly closed, and Ben Carson's lips twitched, making Phyllida aware that his mouth indicated his possession of a sense of humour. 'Seaminster is a small friendly place, and you will know from our local press and the central role the Company plays in your midst–' this time Hutton's eyes rolled – 'about the distressing time we have recently gone through.' Miss Tate's large figure appeared to be undisciplined beneath a not quite roomy enough tent of a dress, and on the word 'distressing' a tremor passed over its various protrusions. 'This, now, is at an end, and the large attendance here tonight is a heartening vote of confidence in our future as well as an indication that Seaminster is aware that our troubles are over. Thank you all very much for being here.'

Miss Tate stopped and gave a slight bow, eliciting a ragged round of applause.

'Thank you.' Her large bosom rose and fell dramatically with the emotion apparent in her suddenly less confident face, and Phyllida decided that Amy Tate really cared about the Little Theatre Company. 'Now.' The attempt to rally was quickly effective. 'I'm going to suggest that those who are here as would-be thespians sit in the front rows, and those interested in stage management go with Barney and Philip here.' Turning, Phyllida was for the first time aware of the two men standing against the wall near the door where she had come in, one tall and middle-aged with a lot of white hair, the other younger and shorter and with a bald crown above a dark close-cropped ring. As Amy Tate stopped speaking the younger one stepped forward, smiling and beckoning, and almost half the audience moved hesitantly out of their seats and followed the men through the door.

'That's right!' commented Miss Tate as the door closed behind them. 'Now, if all you would-be actors and actresses would like to close ranks... Carol?'

Carol Swain rose promptly and descended the stage. She walked well and had a good figure, and Phyllida was aware that among those members of the audience obediently moving forward several of the men had paused to watch her. She, too, picked some papers off a side table, then proceeded to hand them out along the first two rows of seats, which, with the departure of the would-be stage staff, now accommodated all those who remained.

'Thank you, Carol.' Miss Tate was still on her feet. 'Now, you will see there is an extract from *Twelfth Night*, a famous two-hander, for the ladies – the first meeting between the Countess Olivia and Viola – and some even more famous soliloquies for the gentlemen. Perhaps we could begin with two of the ladies.' Miss Tate gave a token half turn towards Henry Hutton, who nodded with the air of weary resignation which Phyllida suspected he had developed as his best defence against Miss Tate's exuberance. 'Now.' Miss Tate went through the motions of combing her audience with her eyes, but Phyllida knew that her glance would come to rest on Sonia Sheridan. 'How about... Perhaps you would read the Countess, Mrs–?'

'Sheridan. Sonia Sheridan. I'd be pleased to.'

'Good! And Viola...' The glance, this time, stopped a few places beyond Phyllida, at a pair of feet in trainers which was all she could see of the woman with whom she could be about to enter a dialogue. 'You, perhaps? Yes, the lady in the white blouse. Miss...?'

'Jones. June Jones.'

The voice was strong, low and resonant. Phyllida liked it, and the other frisson, the one that came while waiting in the wings, shot suddenly through her.

'Right then, Miss Jones, Mrs Sheridan. Off you go, if you will. Page four.'

'Speak to me.' Mrs Sheridan responded, almost eliminating her American accent. 'I shall answer for her.'

'Most radiant, exquisite and unmatchable beauty–'

Phyllida knew the lovely scene by heart, and looked at the paper in her hand merely to disguise the fact. Her knowledge of it enabled her as it progressed to glance up every few seconds and observe the reactions on the stage. In each case they were rapt: Carol Swain and the red-haired man sat motionless, Miss Tate stopped fidgeting, Paul Harvey's face relaxed and Ben Carson's lightened, and Henry Hutton pulled himself upright in his chair and shed his air of lethargy.

'...O! You should not rest
Between the elements of air and earth,
But you should pity me!'

As the applause broke out Phyllida leaned forward to look towards her protagonist at the moment her protagonist leaned forward to look towards her. Both nodded but only Phyllida smiled, and taking in the no-nonsense severity of June Jones's appearance Phyllida had to give Amy Tate credit for recognising such well-hidden talent.

'Bravo!' Miss Tate now boomed, bouncing to her feet. Even Henry Hutton was languidly clapping. 'That was a treat for us all, and I need hardly tell you–' Miss Tate made a token turn towards Hutton, who nodded testily – 'that Mrs Sheridan and Miss Jones are now actor-members of the Little Theatre Company, if they care to accept our invitation to join.' She looked hopefully from Mrs Sheridan to Miss Jones, and from her satisfied smile Phyllida assumed that Miss Jones too had nodded. 'Good. Good. But tell me. You both appear to have had – some experience?'

'I've belonged to societies back home,' Mrs Sheridan drawled, and Phyllida waited with a curiosity as intense as that now featuring in Miss Tate's face as her gaze turned to Miss Jones.

'Only family charades, but I once won an elocution prize.' Miss Jones's everyday voice, though unavoidably attractive, was as brisk as her appearance.

'That doesn't surprise me, Miss Jones.' Miss Tate beamed approvingly before dropping her eyes to the sheets of paper in her hands. 'Now.' She rustled them, turned the page. Anti-climax was likely if the same scene were to be immediately repeated. 'I think something for the men... The great soliloquies from *Hamlet*. Nothing like the deep end, is there?' Miss Tate laughed loudly at her little joke, and there was a nervous titter of response from male members of the audience. 'Perhaps you, the gentleman in the front row with the red tie?'

The gentleman in the front row with the best physique, Phyllida interpreted. But physically appropriate leading men were always hard to come by for amateur companies, and it was as good a point as any to start at when investigating the unknown. In the event, the man read *Oh what a rogue and peasant slave am I!* passably well, and was commended by Miss Tate without the issue of an invitation to join the Company. Two more men read two further *Hamlet* soliloquies to similar standard and with similar response, and a fourth, after stumbling on his first and second lines, mumbled something unintelligible, got to his feet, and fled.

'Oh, dear! Well, we all suffer at some time, even those of us with a lot of experience of acting in public.' Phyllida had to admire the way Miss Tate had somehow contrived to place herself in a category with Dames Judi Dench and Diana Rigg. 'Now, I've got your names, and please give your addresses to our secretary Carol—' a smiling glance to indicate – 'who will be in touch with our decision. Now, I suggest those of you who haven't yet performed might care to act out a scene from Barrie's *Dear Brutus.*' Another token glance towards Henry Hutton elicited another testy nod. 'Barrie is, I suppose, considered nowadays to be rather dated, but he did write some very good parts, and this play I think retains its surreal charm.' Phyllida decided there was more to Miss Tate than bombast. 'So, Henry, would you like to allocate the roles?'

'Not at all, my dear Amy. I leave it to your very competent self.' Neither face nor voice revealed the sarcasm Phyllida was sure was present in the words. 'Except that I suggest the gentleman at the far end of the second row for the puppet master Lob who pulls all the strings.'

Phyllida had played more than one role in *Dear Brutus* over the past two decades, beginning with the dream daughter Margaret and graduating to the mature and sombre Mrs Dearth, whom Barrie describes in his characteristically long and wordy preface as 'a white-faced gypsy with a husky voice, most beautiful when she is sullen and therefore frequently at her best'. Miss Tate cast the rest of her chosen scene without too much difficulty, but after raking the audience with a last thoughtful glance she turned to Sonia Sheridan and asked her if she would be good enough to read Mrs Dearth.

'I was about to suggest that those who have already auditioned might like to go through to the green-room, where there are coffee and biscuits. But if you wouldn't mind, Mrs Sheridan...?'

Mrs Sheridan assured Miss Tate that she would be honoured, and the woman who had played Viola got to her feet and led the Hamlets out of the room.

Some of the acting in the night-time garden scene of *Dear Brutus* would have needed a lot of coaching to make it acceptable, and some was incorrigible. After thanking everyone profusely Miss Tate repeated the suggestion she had made to the Hamlets about leaving addresses, and asked the only two members of the audience who had not yet performed, a man and a woman, if they would care to read the most dramatic of the scenes between Hamlet and his mother, which they would find on the last couple of sheets. Phyllida left the room with the *Dear Brutus* group.

The green-room was now the picture of welcome and cheer. During the auditions the long table against the wall had received a white cloth, on which were cups and saucers, tea and coffee pots, and plates of tasty looking biscuits. Two young women Phyllida hadn't seen before were presiding, and one of them poured her a coffee.

'It's hard to believe you've never been on the professional stage.' Phyllida had been looking without success for her Viola, and had seen the young man now beside her crossing the room with the obvious purpose of speaking to her. He wore horn-rimmed glasses, spoke with precision, and had a scholarly air, heightened by his conventional dress and untrendy hairstyle.

'Thank you. I've played with a few societies back home over the years. I guess you get experience from amateur productions as well as professional.'

'Of course.' The young man blinked, in acknowledgement that he might have sounded condescending, Phyllida thought, and decided he was someone she could like. 'Anyway, congratulations on a lovely performance. I'm so glad you're going to join us.'

'Thank you. Do *you* act? Or are you behind the scenes?'

'I try to act. I'm Kevin Keithley, by the way.'

'Kevin Keithley.' Phyllida repeated the name to give herself time to absorb her shock, which within a few seconds she realised was a pleasant one. If Jenny hadn't shown her in a myriad ways that she was a strong-minded young woman with surprisingly conventional principles, she might have suspected that Kevin Keithley's interest in her was not in Jenny's. But Jenny being the tough young soul Phyllida believed her to be, it looked like she could have attracted him via more than her obvious charms. And that her taste in men was maturing. 'And I know you're Mrs Sheridan.'

'Sonia.'

'Thank you. Sonia. Ah, here they come. I don't think Henry looks too happy, but it isn't easy to tell. And Amy is ever-optimistic.'

Amy Tate called for quiet, and gave a brief, 'Don't ring us, we'll ring you' admonition to the assembly in general before announcing that the rest of the evening, 'Exactly–' looking at her watch – 'half an hour,' would be given over to socialising.

Then she joined Phyllida and Kevin.

'I must congratulate you personally, Mrs Sheridan, on a splendid performance. It's hard to believe you've never been on the professional stage.'

Phyllida and Kevin exchanged expressionless looks.

'Thank you. Well, I guess I've done enough amateur to pick up a few tips.'

'You certainly have! Now tell me, which part of America do you come from?'

Phyllida recited the relevant part of Sonia's biography with few fears of being picked up on it: Amy Tate, having secured her prize, had an eye and an ear trained elsewhere. But she did ask for Mrs Sheridan's Seaminster address.

'I'm living at your Golden Lion at the moment. I guess I don't know yet if I'll be staying long enough to put down roots.'

'The Golden Lion! Our most historic and prestigious hotel!' Sonia Sheridan had regained all of Miss Tate's attention. 'Now,' she went on eagerly, 'Henry and I will be casting our next production on Monday, and we do so hope you can come along. You too, Kevin,' she added, with less enthusiasm.

Kevin and Sonia both nodded as Henry Hutton, cup and saucer in hand, strolled up to them. 'That was well done,' he told Sonia. Phyllida could see no approbation in his face. 'I hope Amy has been inviting you to Monday night's casting.'

'She has. And I look forward to it.' Feeling a bit sorry for Jenny's boyfriend, Phyllida turned to him. 'So, I gather, does this young man.'

'Yes. Good. Amy–' Henry turned with obvious reluctance to Miss Tate. 'I need a word.' 'Word' was spoken with a slight emphasis, and Phyllida was intrigued to see

78

Amy Tate's various excrescences quiver in what looked like excitement.

'Of course, Henry.' Even Mrs Sheridan was taking second place. 'Shall we ... ? Excuse us,' she offered hastily, and moved away at Henry Hutton's side, having difficulty, Phyllida noticed with amusement, in slowing her bustling stride to his languid progress.

'Sounds intriguing,' Mrs Sheridan drawled.

'Oh, they're always in a huddle, and I don't need to tell you I don't mean in any romantic sense.' Kevin grinned at her. 'I think they must have some guilty secret in common. They and some of the others. You come across them with their heads together, and they leap apart.'

'Gracious. You don't think... This drugs business? But surely not now, and not Miss Tate!'

Kevin Keithley shrugged. 'I don't suppose so. They're probably collaborating on writing the play of the century, or something.'

'That'll be it.' Phyllida caught sight of June Jones, studying one of the exhibition pictures on the wall near the door out to the foyer. Miss Tate and Henry Hutton were in earnest conversation just beyond her, so she had two reasons to move on.

'I've just spotted my Viola,' she excused herself, 'and I'd like to congratulate her. I look forward to seeing you on Monday, Kevin.'

Glad to have a favourable report for Jenny, Phyllida strolled across the room, passing the rapt June Jones and stopping by a picture at right angles which might just put her within earshot of Amy Tate and Henry Hutton.

It was a disappointment to be able to make out no more than murmurs, but as she stood with her eyes fixed unseeingly on an unattractive shriek of a painting Carol Swain came up to the door and stopped beside them.

'All fixed up?' she asked. She, too, spoke in a lowered voice, and Phyllida could only just hear her.

'Yes. The ninth at eleven thirty. The long-range forecast is good.' To hear Amy Tate use such hushed, conspiratorial tones – and speak in code? – was so dramatically un-expected the adrenaline surged again. 'You'll inform the others?'

'Never fear. Well, see you on Monday, if not before.' Carol spoke her last sentence loud, clear and cheerful, and left the room followed by Henry Hutton. Miss Tate moved back into the centre, and Phyllida strolled across to June Jones, still apparently absorbed in another visible affront.

'You made that piece from *Twelfth Night* very enjoyable,' Sonia murmured, and the woman gave a little start of shock. 'I'm sorry, you were miles away, weren't you? Do you really *like* that picture?'

'No.' June Jones turned to her with a slight smile. 'I just find it interesting why someone should want to paint it, and someone else should want to hang it on a wall. Yes, that was a good dialogue.'

'And everyone's been telling you they can hardly believe you've never been on the professional stage? Sorry, perhaps you have.'

'No. But I haven't really spoken to any-one.'

'Ah. You'll come to the casting, though, on Monday?'

'I'll come to that, yes.'

'Good. Perhaps we'll get to play together in the new production.'

'Perhaps. Good-night.' With another brief stretch of the lips June Jones disappeared through the door, a moment before Miss Tate clapped her hands for silence and told everyone the caretaker would be wanting to lock up and it was time to bring a fruitful evening to a close.

Promptly obedient, Phyllida followed Miss Jones out to the foyer, where she rang for a taxi to take her back to the Golden Lion and the temporary annihilation of Sonia Sheridan.

## Five

A light was shining from a second floor window across Dawlish Square when Phyllida stepped out of her taxi in front of the Golden Lion, and when she had paid the driver and he had driven away she crossed the floodlit garden path, skirted the imposing statue of Seaminster's eponymous benefactor and let herself into the office building. As she entered the Agency Peter came out of the rest room smiling his pleasure and smoothing his ruffled hair. Sometimes when she called in at night he was still at his desk, and sometimes he had obviously been lying on the big soft sofa which was the rest room's centrepiece. Phyllida knew that his live-in girlfriend had left him soon after she had come to work for the Agency, and sometimes he made gloomy comments when they were on their own about the failure of other would-be relationships that had appeared promising, but neither of them had ever commented on the long hours he spent in the office. Phyllida believed he just liked the place, and it was certainly civilised and comfortable, with its small modern kitchen and magnificent Victorian bathroom. Jenny had been responsible for transforming the kitchen from the stone sink and cold tap that had been its sole contents when Peter leased the suite of rooms, but he had firmly withstood her eagerness to do likewise for what he always referred to as the king of bathrooms.

'It was a pleasant, worthy, to-be-expected kind of an evening,' Phyllida told him as they took their usual places in his office, 'until the last few minutes. And I'm wondering if I manufactured a conspiracy then because of being so anxious to find one.'

'Not you. Carry on.'

His eyes sparkling, Peter reached out and down to what Phyllida had once assumed to be a filing cabinet, and extracted bottles of Scotch and soda and a couple of good glasses.

'It was someone else, anyway – Jenny's boyfriend Kevin – who remarked on the conspiratorial way Henry Hutton came up and asked Miss Tate for "a word" when the three of us were talking in the green-room after the auditions. When they'd moved off together he told me they were always in a huddle and suggested jokily that they might have a guilty secret. "They and some of the others" is what he said; I'll put it all down in my report in the morning. Mrs Sheridan was shocked by the thought that it might be drugs still, but Kevin laughed off that idea. Which my own common sense tells me to do as well: Amy Tate at least is the last person in the world you'd put down as being mixed up with drug dealing, she looked more as if she was planning a midnight feast in the dorm. But there's certainly something in the offing, Peter. I saw Miss Tate and Hutton move over to the door, so Mrs Sheridan excused herself from Kevin Keithley and was able to stroll into partial earshot. Carol Swain – Ben Carson's girl-friend – had joined them and they were talking unnaturally quietly. But I did hear Carol ask if it was all fixed up, and Amy Tate tell her in a very uncharacteristic whisper that it was. Miss Tate also told her it was the ninth at eleven thirty, and that the long-range forecast was good. No indication of a.m. or p.m.'

'Night-time sounds more likely in view of the huddle, but you never know. "The long range forecast is good",' Peter repeated musingly. 'Code? Or simply indicating some outdoor activity? If it's to do with drug dealing it'll have to be code.'

'That was my thought. Then Carol agreed to "inform the others", and they went their ways. One thing...' Phyllida shivered, then shook her head, smiling as Peter glanced anxiously towards the near window. 'If the conspiracy *is* to do with drugs, there was something chilling in the gleeful, childlike sort of attitude of Miss Tate, as if she was in line for a treat. Something – something amoral, as if it was *fun* to be still getting away with it despite the recent police intervention and the arrest. But obviously there could be a hundred other explanations. All I know is that some kind of conspiracy's afoot among some members of the Little Theatre Company. No evidence so far that it's to do with drugs, or that Paul Harper – or Ben Carson – has any part in it. "The others" could mean the company as a whole, some members of it, or I suppose it could mean people nothing to do with the society at all.'

'It could. Anyway, I'll tell Harper senior that my operative is in place and hasn't – as yet – found any evidence that his son is involved in anything to do with drugs. That's truth enough. And the ninth ... July?'

'It's the next ninth.'

'Even without any evidence so far that our subject is involved, I think Miss Bowden or Steve should be waiting outside one of three homes early on Wednesday morning, follow its occupant when he or she leaves, and resume vigil towards evening if nothing unusual happens at eleven thirty a.m.'

'Perhaps they'll just converge on the theatre.'

'Whatever the person you're following does at eleven thirty a.m. try to keep close. You can follow him or her into the theatre on a very small pretext.'

'True. What about Steve and me both, covering two homes?'

'That would ease the odds in our favour. We'll discuss the mechanics with Steve. Did Mrs Sheridan make the usual impact?'

'Yes.' Phyllida discovered that she wasn't going to tell Peter about Steve's visit to the Golden Lion. Nor about the contrast between Miss Tate's reaction tonight and her reaction the first time she had seen Phyllida Moon. 'I arrived in a small group and Miss Tate directed all her chat at Sonia. And selected her as her first reader. Olivia in *Twelfth Night,* with an unlikely-looking but what turned out to be splendid Viola. We earned a burst of spontaneous applause.'

'Good for you. Unlikely-looking?'

'No evidence of personal vanity. Name of June Jones. Full marks to Amy Tate for spotting her potential, she had a remarkable voice and knew how to use it. It was really exciting, Peter.'

'You never know the perks this job will provide. I remember... No, another time. Did you speak to this June Jones afterwards?'

'For a moment, at the end of the socialising. She was standing the other side of the door when I went to eavesdrop on Hutton and Co, and when they dispersed I went up to her – she was looking at one of the pictures in a terrible exhibition on the green-room walls. We only exchanged a few words, Sonia-led, and then she left. But at least she told me she was coming to next Monday's casting. We're to do a play by Henry Hutton, one he told Sonia he sets more store by than the current production.'

'Is he a navel gazer?'

'I'd say he has a good sense of self-worth. He made me think of the old actor-manager breed, Beerbohm Tree and so on. My guess would be that he isn't interested in women. His reactions don't show in his face, which is unnerving. I'd also say there's some jostling for position between him and Amy Tate – two egotists with comically different styles. She's helping to cast his play, so I anticipate some sparks, although they've been working together for some time I gather, so they must be able to rub along. I could imagine her being kind and even warm – if her conspiratorial glee wasn't to do with drugs – but never Henry Hutton. I'll put it all down.'

'What was your impression of Jenny's Kevin?' Peter refilled the glasses.

'I could like him. He's untrendy and very polite, not a type I should have thought would make it – or want to make it – with Jenny. He appears to have an objective view of life with the Little Theatre Company, and I suspect a becoming modesty. He'll be at the casting too.'

'You didn't speak to Paul Harper or Ben Carson?'

'I'm sorry, no. The time allowed for

socialising after the auditions was a strict half hour, and – well, Sonia Sheridan is the sort of woman who gets sought out before she has a chance to do much seeking.' It was absurd to feel uncomfortably immodest about someone who didn't exist. 'Though as I said, I did excuse myself to Kevin Keithley when I saw Miss Tate and Hutton with their heads together near the door. I was talking to June Jones when Miss Tate made her final announcement of the evening: that it was over and would we mind going home. But I'll get a chance on Monday, and beyond.'

'Of course you will. And you did wonders in that half hour. How did young Harper and his friend strike you from a distance?'

'Harper's a golden boy, but there's no doubt he's ill at ease with himself, although he made an effort to respond when anyone spoke to him. His friend Ben Carson could be one of those people who look rather dour on the surface but turn out to have a dry sense of humour; I thought I saw it in the set of his mouth. I also got the feeling he wasn't a happy man, although that again could just be my anxiety for people and things not to be straightforward. His fiancée, Carol Swain, was in evidence –

she's the company secretary. Blonde, beautiful, and obviously intelligent. The golden girl, but too sophisticated as well as too old for Harper, and I didn't get any feeling of rivalry between the two men. Amy Tate is the archetypal jolly hockey sticks, but it was she who was shrewd enough to spot the talents of the dour Miss Jones. There was a red-haired man on the platform I can't tell you anything about as yet, not even impressions because he was as stingy with facial expressions as Henry Hutton. There'll be more next time.'

'You've done pretty well this time.' Peter turned to look at his wall clock. 'Don't come in tomorrow until you really feel like it.'

'Aren't you in London in the morning?'

'Yes. But Jenny'll be able to cope.' The expression in the bright brown eyes was at variance with the reassurance in the voice.

'Probably. But she'll cope better with some help, and I think it's time I aired a consistent Mary Bowden.'

'Not much fun, eh?'

'More of a test of ingenuity than Mandy. But I'd rather be at work during the working day.' With less opportunity for thoughts about Sunday's Open Day at the Botanical Gardens than there would be working alone in house or garden, or sitting in the library trying to write her ongoing history of women and the theatre.

'That's great, then. Thanks. I'll be back in the early afternoon.'

Sonia Sheridan offered her second salute of the evening to the bronze rendition of Sir Charles Dawlish, JP, MP, exchanged a few good-night words with the two girls in the Golden Lion's reception, then strolled up the elegant main staircase. Half an hour later Phyllida descended the back stairs and drove home. Attempting to analyse a sensation of wistfulness she was aware of as she climbed her own stairs to bed, she was amused to realise that it was nostalgia, awakened by her reading of the scene from *Twelfth Night*. It seemed a long time since she had played a live stage role with other actors she had no power to hurt or deceive, and experienced the unique but simple satisfaction of knowing she was playing it well.

The morning was warm, calm and clear, and with no props to carry beyond the few needed to give Mary Bowden her own persona, Phyllida decided to walk into town her favourite way – along the Parade – and savour the lazy sparkle of the sea. Seaminster was nearing the peak of its decorous summer influx, and the out-of-season resident stalwarts with their dogs, many well enough known now to Phyllida for a word of greeting in passing, were in the minority to the young families and little groups of boys and girls slopping on and off the pavements.

In her room at the Golden Lion, her undramatic transformation was almost complete when the telephone rang.

'A call for Mrs Sheridan, Miss Moon.' John Bright's team at the hotel were so well schooled to cope with Agency business Phyllida had no worries about an open line. 'I said I thought she might have gone out, but I'd try her room. Is she there?'

'What sort of voice, Linda?'

'Loud. Female.'

'Ah. Put her through, will you? First, though: a Miss Mary Bowden *will* soon be going out.'

Amy Tate was profuse in her apologies for possibly disturbing Mrs Sheridan. 'But I – we – just thought – as you're living in a hotel at the moment, which even when it's our lovely Golden Lion can't feel *quite* like home – tonight is the night in the week when members tend to come into the green-room for a coffee and a chat. Nothing special, just that Friday seems to suit most of us, and so people tend to drift in. It was just a thought, Mrs Sheridan. Everyone's still talking about that lovely dialogue between you and Miss Jones. I'd like to contact her, too, but with our electing you both to membership immediately she didn't leave her address–'

'She told me she's coming to the casting on Monday, so don't worry. About tonight, I guess I'd like that very much. What time do you tend to forgather?'

'Oh, any time from eight o'clock. Just for an hour or so. I think it's good for our team-work on stage as well as fun for us to be sociable.'

'I'm sure.'

'So we'll hope to see you at around eight o'clock this evening. The Appleby Players have a production on this week, so the outside doors will be open.'

'Do other companies use the green-room?'

'Oh, no!' Mrs Sheridan could have made an indecent suggestion. 'What we call the green-room and the rehearsal room are for the Society's exclusive use. We're very long-established, you know, and the disposition of the premises is vested in us. Use of the theatre by other companies is in our gift.

There's a good-sized room and another set of lavatories on the ground floor, and other companies use those.'

'So I'm among the élite!' Mrs Sheridan's comment, and her subsequent laugh, were without sarcasm, and Phyllida heard Amy Tate's contented murmur. 'Well, I look forward to it. Thank you for the invitation.'

Grinning at her reflection in her dressing-table mirror, Phyllida sat down in front of it to complete her transformation. She had glanced into it intermittently while talking, and been amused to hear Mrs Sheridan's sophisticated drawl emerging from the pursed, pale lips of Mary Bowden, whose wary expression she had started to assume before the telephone rang.

Starting to think seriously about Miss Bowden the night before, Phyllida had realised that to date she was nothing beyond her name. This at least offered a clean slate on which to write, but the scope was limited: Miss Bowden must continue negative, except for her ability to convey a sense that her clients – including perhaps Chief Superintendent Kendrick – were in safe and sensible hands.

Phyllida's sallow skin tanned painlessly and quickly with very little exposure to the sun, and the couple of sessions she had had in the garden had been enough to start the process delayed this year by her two months in London commuting by tube between studio and flat. So Miss Bowden's putty-coloured complexion, combined with her guarded face and her no-nonsense French pleat, added up to a transformation Phyllida was relieved to see was after all as dramatic in its way as the transformation into Mandy. She had not liked the thought that there might be something of Mary Bowden already present.

When she had nodded cool approval into the glass Phyllida left her room and descended the back stairs, then walked through to Reception, where she paused as usual for the first test of her metamorphosis.

She passed it. Linda asked her what she could do for her, and went on looking politely helpful until Phyllida let her own smile break fleetingly through.

'Ah.' Linda smiled too. 'Miss Bowden. If anyone rings, shall I say when you'll be back?'

'I should think in the early afternoon.' It was Miss Bowden's flat, slightly northern voice. 'Whoever rings – and whoever they're ringing – please take a note and tell them their call will be returned.'

Spurred by her relief that Steve and Jenny also failed to recognise her, Phyllida was unable to resist playing a game with them, pretending to be the would-be client they had taken her for. It was only when she was eventually unable to hide her own smile that Jenny gave a shout, and Steve banged his fist against his head.

'Bloody idiots!' he yelled. 'We were expecting you! For heaven's sake don't tell Peter, Phyllida, or he'll decide I'm in the wrong job.'

'You don't feel the same attraction you feel towards Mrs Sheridan?' Phyllida asked in her own voice. 'Ah, well, never mind. Now' – it was Miss Bowden speaking – 'I'll be in the general office if any would-be clients appear, and you can go out for your lunchtime sandwich, Jenny, if you feel like it. I think I can cope in Reception.'

Jenny's face lit up. 'Thanks, Phyllida!'

'Miss Bowden. Better get used to it.'

'Yes, of course. Sorry. I've brought my lunch, Miss Bowden, but it'd be great to eat it by the sea.'

'Mrs Sheridan's been invited to the dramatic society's green-room tonight for a little socialising.' While she looked like Mary

Bowden, Phyllida decided, she must sound like her, even if there was no outsider present. But when she was alone with the Agency staff she would allow the content of what she said to be her own. 'Might be interesting.'

Phyllida caught and held Steve's eyes, which had been anxious since her first mention of Mrs Sheridan, and smiled her own reassuring smile as he abandoned his habitual support of the doorframe and drew a deep defensive breath. Jenny had glanced down at a paper on the reception counter, and Phyllida offered him a shake of the head, still smiling.

'Just might,' Steve agreed, relapsing with relief.

'Haven't you anywhere to go?' Phyllida asked him, immediately regretting the question as Steve stiffened again. She should have remembered his simplistic approach to life, which would make him suspect her of threatening to exact a price for her silence.

'Yes,' he said sullenly, moving slowly towards the door. Phyllida felt helpless as she watched him, but the telephone came to her aid. When Jenny answered it and then started rummaging for something below the counter, she followed Steve and checked him in the open doorway.

'I'm only interested,' she whispered in her own voice. 'You should know me by now, Steve.'

It came out as a reproach, and to her relief Steve relaxed again and gave her one of his rare smiles. 'Yeah, I reckon. Sorry. I'm still after Jim McGregor, but he never appears before ten. Hope Mrs Sheridan has a lovely evening.'

'Thanks, Steve.'

As the door closed Jenny's face was immediately pleading.

'You met Kevin. What did you think of him? Did you like him?'

'I met him and I liked him. Truly. And his reaction to Miss Tate and Mr Hutton going into a huddle ... well, if they're up to something, Jenny, I don't see him being part of it. So – so far, so good.'

'Oh, Phyllida! Miss Bowden. Thanks!'

'If you care for people, Jenny, you have to trust them.'

Closing her face to accord with her growing knowledge of Miss Bowden, Phyllida gave Jenny a measured smile and went into the general office, where she read *The Times* and some of Peter's improving detective agency literature, interrupted twice by Jenny: first with a cup of coffee and, half an hour later, by the announcement that there was a would-be client at the counter.

As Peter had suggested, Phyllida led the woman into his office, having to force herself to overcome her diffidence as for the first time she sat in his chair and motioned someone else to sit in hers. The woman was distraught and needed the professionally soothing approach Miss Bowden was able to provide, but her problem appeared to be a straightforward job for Steve: checking up on a husband she believed to be straying. Phyllida took notes, and when the woman had finished she told her after only an instant's hesitation that the Agency would accept the case. But some trepidation had crept up on her by the time Peter got back, and it was a relief to see him nod and smile when she had shown him her notes and told him what she had done.

'We didn't discuss whether you wanted me to say yea or nay. But this seems straightforward.'

'So it does. And you took the right initiative. If there'd been anything iffy or unusually complex you'd have told the woman you'd have to refer things to me.'

'I would.'

He was studying her. 'So we meet Miss Bowden at last. I was afraid – forgive me – that she might be you, but she isn't.'

'Thank you!'

'She's someone, though. Full marks yet again. Was it difficult?'

'Not as difficult as I was afraid it might be. Now, Mrs Sheridan's been invited to socialise at the Little Theatre this evening; apparently Friday night is friendship night.'

'Great!' The expressive face lit up. 'So as you'll be working tonight you'll be taking the afternoon off. That's an order.'

'All right.' She would walk, Phyllida decided. Take the car to another stretch of shore, and walk. She hadn't walked for more than two months, and suddenly it was what she wanted to do, more than anything in the world apart from standing for the second time as herself in front of Dr Jack Pusey.

# Six

When Sonia Sheridan entered the green-room at the Little Theatre she found Amy Tate, Carol Swain, and the two young men already settled in and drinking coffee. Miss Tate was sitting with the red-haired man who had been on the platform the night of the auditions, and rising with a gratified smile she hastened across the room to welcome Mrs Sheridan and introduce her companion as he got to his feet.

'This is Clive Simpson, Sonia, our treasurer and our absolute prop and mainstay.'

'Treasure as well as treasurer,' Mrs Sheridan murmured, placing her fingers for a moment against the palm of the hand Clive Simpson had thrust forward.

'You gave an excellent reading of Olivia,' he told her, the briskness of his voice matching his neat, spare appearance and the gunlike rigidity of his extended hand.

'Well, thank you.' Mrs Sheridan was smiling her thanks as well, but Clive Simpson continued to look serious. 'It's a lovely exchange and it was good to be reading it aloud again. Miss Jones was a wonderful Viola.'

'I hope she'll keep her promise to appear on Monday,' Amy Tate said anxiously. 'Now. Coffee? Tea?' The hand on her arm had Phyllida turning towards the table, now clothless, on which were urn, coffee pot and a few hopeful rows of cups and saucers.

'Coffee, please. Black. No sugar.' Phyllida tried to eat and drink in public what she felt accorded with her current character, but there were limits. None of her creations took sugar.

'There we are!' Miss Tate had poured the coffee herself, and handed it over with a flourish.

'Thank you.' Clive Simpson, walking with short, quick steps, was on his way out of the room. 'So tell me about your wonderful treasurer. What does he do when he isn't looking after the Little Theatre Company?'

'He's an accountant. White and Simpson in Dale Street. A long-established firm with a nice old frontage. You may have noticed it?'

'No. But Mr Simpson seems a little like an old-fashioned gentleman.'

Miss Tate considered. 'I *was* surprised

when his wife told me the other week that she was taking him out for a forty-fifth birthday dinner,' she conceded. 'I'd always assumed he was well over fifty. Angela Simpson, now, she's just the opposite; she's someone who'll always seem young. I wonder sometimes how they ever got together. Now, who else should you meet?'

'Just everyone,' Sonia suggested, turning towards the three young people sitting together and all seeming less than cheerful. Paul Harper was staring down into his coffee cup, Ben Carson was looking gravely from him to Carol, and Carol, her face anxious, had her hand up to Paul's.

'Come on, Paul,' Phyllida heard her coax, eyes and ears alert behind Mrs Sheridan's lazy smile. 'What's the matter? No exams are worth so much angst.'

'He worries about them far too much,' Ben Carson said. His voice suited him, deep and measured.

Paul's head shot up. 'I can't help it,' he said, looking at Ben with an expression of entreaty Phyllida was unable to interpret. 'So much hangs on how I do.'

'Carol! Ben! Paul!' Amy Tate's loud rallying tones put paid to the conversation they cut into. 'Here's Mrs Sheridan! It's so good she felt she could join us tonight.'

Ben Carson said, 'Hi!' and got immediately to his feet. After a few seconds Paul followed suit, mumbling a greeting, and Carol looked up with a bright smile.

'Hello again!' she said. 'Good to see you.' She indicated the empty chair at the table, but before Sonia could accept it Miss Tate rejected it on her behalf with a wave of the hand.

'Thank you, Carol, but we must circulate!' she declared. 'It's such a good opportunity for Sonia to meet as many of our members as possible.'

'Are you expecting Mr Hutton tonight?' Sonia enquired as they approached the next occupied table.

'Not tonight.' The response was a contented purr. 'He is, he told us, entertaining. One of his little suppers. If we are to believe Henry, they are gastronomic treats.' A statement Amy Tate had indicated she personally could neither confirm nor deny. 'These Friday nights are very informal, you know, no one is ever expected to be here, apart from whoever volunteers to make the tea and coffee.'

'A fine institution. Is this a typical attendance?'

'Oh, yes.'

There were perhaps twenty people in the room, standing about or sitting at the small tables, and Amy Tate introduced the new member to them all. Phyllida was amused to meet her favourite librarian from the reference library where she sat and worked on her book as often as she could, and to experience again what was no longer a phenomenon: someone she knew looking at her as a stranger.

'So no one else who came for the auditions is here tonight,' she commented mischievously, as to her relief Miss Tate began to steer her back towards her subjects.

'Well, no.' The deep-set eyes veered away. 'We're only just getting round to informing those we are inviting to join the Company. Next week, perhaps, or the week after.' *It doesn't really matter*, Phyllida interpreted. *The auditions yielded us our prize: you and, we hope, Miss Jones.* At least there was one area where the co-Chairs were in agreement.

'Do join us,' Ben Carson suggested, as Amy and Sonia came back into earshot, getting to his feet again and swivelling a fifth chair from the adjoining table. With a little manoeuvring – Miss Tate required more than her share of the space available at the table for four – the five of them sat down in an uneven circle.

'This is a very civilised green-room,' Mrs Sheridan commented, smiling round on them. 'You're really fortunate. Some of the amateur set-ups I've seen, here and back home!'

'I know.' Amy Tate purred again. 'We do appreciate it.'

'And the fact that we can have it to ourselves and despatch other companies to the ground floor,' Carol said, with a triumphant little laugh. 'Not that they're deprived. There's almost as much space down there as we have up here.'

Ben Carson asked Sonia if she knew the history of the theatre, and when she said she had only a vague idea he succinctly filled her in, his face lightening and animating as he spoke and his turn of phrase confirming his possession of the sense of humour she thought she had already seen lurking about his mouth.

'It must have been a fabulous store,' Sonia commented as, with a glance at his fiancée, Carson fell silent and the usual grave look reclaimed his face.

'There are photos all over the place,' Carol

said. 'Faded sepia. Another world.'

'And how are you tonight, Paul?' Amy asked, with a show of concern which Phyllida thought was genuine.

'I'm fine.' Paul flushed an instant crimson, which almost as quickly ebbed.

'Worrying about his exams,' Carol supplied.

'I wish you wouldn't keep reminding me!' He turned a disgruntled look from Carol to Ben.

'Sorry!' they said in unison.

'No, well ... I'm all right.' But Phyllida could see the effort in the sudden deep breath and the fleeting closure of the large blue eyes as Paul Harper leaned across to her. 'That was a super reading the other night,' he said, unable to suppress a tacit 'So there!' as again he glanced from Carol to Ben. Paul Harper was clearly not a youth at ease, but studying his face as well as she could in the cosily low light, Phyllida could see no sign in it of the drug abuse Peter had taught her to look for, and none in the faces of the other two young ones. But then, if they were dealing she wouldn't expect to find any.

'Tell me about yourselves,' Sonia invited. 'You, Carol. Are you studying? Or do you have a job?'

'Carol works for an architect,' Amy Tate answered for the girl enthusiastically. 'She has a very responsible–'

'Thanks, Amy.' Carol hadn't hesitated to appropriate her own question, confirming Phyllida's impression of self-assurance. 'I *am* an architect, actually, but only just. Liverpool, last summer. I was lucky to get with Cranmer and Leigh for my first job, but of course so far I'm pretty lowly.'

'Not for long.' Looking into the bright, intelligent eyes Phyllida meant what Sonia had said. 'It's a gruel on both sides of the Atlantic and I know several would-be architects who didn't stay the course.' Phyllida knew one, and wondered fleetingly about the effect of the latitude a character gave her to embellish or neaten her own experience on her own truth. 'And what about you two boys?'

'I have an art gallery,' Ben told her, with his sudden radiant smile. Amy Tate, after a gulping breath, managed to remain silent. 'Here in Seaminster. Not a trendy one, though we do nurture one or two moderns.'

'That I would like. And you, Paul?'

'Hasn't everyone made it plain? A levels.'

'I don't know your subjects.'

'Sorry. No, of course you don't.' The boy was making another effort. 'History, English and Maths. I'm hoping for Oxford, to read Law.'

'Spanning the cultures,' Carol said, smiling encouragingly at Paul. 'That's bright.'

'You have to span them in architecture,' Ben said, and Phyllida noted the flush of pleasure briefly suffusing Carol's cool as he reached for her hand.

'You're three clever young people.' Sonia could drawl things like that without being embarrassing. It was one of the things about her Phyllida enjoyed.

'Now it's your turn,' Carol said. 'Amy tells me you're living at the Golden Lion.'

Phyllida felt she already knew Amy Tate well enough to have no doubts she would have told everyone who had been present at the auditions, given the opportunity. 'Staying there. I don't know just at the moment how long I'll be here in Seaminster.' Phyllida went through Sonia's background, with the further invention, in the light of the serious approach to life being taken by the three young people so earnestly regarding her, that she had worked at one time as an interior designer. 'No solid training. It just

109

sort of happened and one day I had a clientele... Now tell me. Do any of your members do other things together? Like going to other theatres, expeditions, special interest groups?'

There was no doubt she had made more impact than her words warranted. Ben Carson drew a noticeable breath. Paul's head, which had dropped down again towards his coffee cup, shot back up. Carol was looking warily at Amy.

'Some of us have gone in a group to the Chichester Theatre,' Ben said. 'A few times. That's all.' He emphasised the last two words, joining Carol and Paul in looking at Amy Tate, whose face was an odd mixture of timidity and excitement. The excitement Phyllida had seen there the last time she had been in the Little Theatre green-room. And she had just learned that Ben Carson and Paul Harper were part of it too.

There was a moment's silence, and then Amy heaved herself to her feet. 'You seem comfortably settled, Sonia,' she said when she was upright, 'so I think I'll do a little more circulating. I'll see you again before you go.'

Miss Tate did not make the promise in a significant tone of voice, but she had scarcely moved away when Ben Carson said he had forgotten to ask her something he needed to know, excused himself, and followed her across the room. Phyllida's chair was placed so that she could watch him reach her and say a few quiet words. Miss Tate listened, made a slight protesting gesture, then as Ben continued speaking Phyllida saw her various protruberances sag with her shoulders as she nodded, put a hand on his arm, nodded again more vigorously, and went on her way. Ben looked after her for a few seconds before coming back to the table. As he sat down Phyllida had no doubt Paul and Carol were studying his expression, perhaps because both were making an attempt to disguise the fact.

'That's all right,' he said, turning to Sonia with a smile.

'Do you have a role in the Company's administration?' Sonia enquired.

It was a disappointment when he nodded, diluting Phyllida's hope that what Ben Carson had had to say to Amy Tate was personal. 'I'm on the casting committee at the moment. A tricky place to be.'

'I can imagine.'

The rest of the evening passed in similar smooth but superficial vein, and following the first departures Mrs Sheridan got to her feet.

'I think I'll be on my way, too. Thank you for such a nice welcome. I'll look forward to seeing you all again on Monday.' The three of them nodded. 'And now I must just say good-night to Amy.'

Who was there before Phyllida could move away from the table, thanking Mrs Sheridan fulsomely for coming and expressing her pleasure that they would meet again so soon.

Peter lay down on the rest room sofa to try and sleep off his uncomfortable memory of his evening. For once he would have chosen to go back to his small flat and turn in for the night with a double Scotch, but despite his depression he was still curious to know how Phyllida's evening had turned out, and the only way to do this was to remain in the Agency with a light showing in his office windows.

In and out of a light doze he glumly contemplated the immediate past. It was Jenny who had insisted he use his title of doctor – bestowed with his PhD in Crime Fiction – as head of the Agency, and this was the second occasion that a would-be girlfriend had assumed it to be medical and acted as if he was a coward or a liar when he was unable to recommend the right form of treatment for someone knocked unconscious by a fall down a flight of stairs.

Fortunately his inadequacy had remained a private matter, as the crowd through which the girl had attempted to urge him was an impenetrable press of people transfixed by the sudden hold-up caused by the fall ahead of them in the queue leaving the film theatre.

It was the cry, 'Is there a doctor?' that had galvanised her.

'Go on!' she had urged. 'Push through! I'll help you.' Looking at her adorable flushed face and sparkling eyes, he could have sworn that the words 'My hero' would be the next on her lips.

But for the second time in his romantic career he had had to stand there saying he was sorry but he wasn't that kind of doctor, and pray that she wouldn't ask him at that point what kind of a doctor he was, piling bathos on disillusion.

She didn't, but the question of course came later, during a dinner in which she told him her father and mother were both doctors of medicine and how much she enjoyed the company of other medically qualified people.

'*Crime fiction!* A doctorate in crime fiction? It's like – like a doctorate in volleyball!'

'Which is, I believe, to be had in America,' he had responded with cold dignity, feeling very slightly better as he decided that the girl lacked tact. 'You don't care for the genre, then?' Peter considered himself monumentally unlucky not yet to have encountered a girl who both attracted him and was addicted to crime novels.

She had shrugged, and as he shifted his position on the sofa he tried to comfort himself with the memory that at the same time her mouth had pursed, giving her a very mean look.

It wasn't this particular girl, Peter decided as he sat up, it was his love life generally, or rather the current lack of it. A pity, perhaps, that he and Phyllida didn't think of one another that way. Though if they did, of course, he reflected as he got wearily to his feet, it would destroy the best friendship and working relationship he had ever had with a woman. Wandering through to the kitchen he wondered idly if she had a love life. She was so private a person he could never ask her, but he realised he didn't particularly want to know.

He was at his office window when her taxi dropped her, and she acknowledged him discreetly before crossing the square.

'How did it go?' he asked, when they were settled in their usual places and he was leaning down to his drinks cupboard.

'Interestingly. Some things I noticed could be significant, but they could be my fevered imagination because of so much wanting to discover something. It's a working hazard, Peter.'

'I know. But tell me what you might have noticed.'

Phyllida broached her drink, then told him about the tension at the table where the young ones had sat. 'It could just have been Paul and his exam nerves getting to them all, but I had the feeling the other two were at odds in some way, too. I don't necessarily mean with each other, more perhaps as if they all three were jittery about the same thing. Oh, that sounds so vague and in-substantial. As I said, I could have been imagining it. I don't know them.'

'True. But I've already experienced your talent for interpreting nuance.'

'Thank you. Amy Tate was in her element in the absence of Henry Hutton, and she does do it all very well. She's so open and straightforward, so absolutely unsubtle, the more I try to think of her as a clandestine dealer in hard drugs the more absurd it seems. But there is *something* up. When I asked if members of the Company ever formed special interest groups I could see that Carson and Carol Swain, at least, were terrified she might spill some beans. Carson even went after her when she left, I'm sure to warn her to keep quiet... Anything you want me to do tomorrow?'

On Saturdays and Sundays all members of staff kept their mobiles to hand and switched on, but unless something urgent overrode the sanctity of the weekend only Peter went into the office.

'Not as things appear at the moment. Haven't you got anything of your own on?'

The question was a carryover from his recent thoughts and he immediately regretted it; his instinct told him that their rare understanding depended on the strict maintenance of boundaries. It was a relief that she answered him quite readily.

'A friend from London fancies some sea air, so I'll be showing off Seaminster.'

'Nice.'

'It's always nice introducing friends to

116

places one loves.'

'You love Seaminster?'

Phyllida smiled her surprise. 'I didn't know I was going to say that. But yes, I do.'

'So do I. Have a good time.'

Ralph Harding had tried a couple of times to invite himself to visit her, and at his second request Phyllida had given in, feeling it would be easier to keep things the way she wanted them with the promise of Sunday at the Botanical Gardens. Easier – but not easy, with the task of conveying the lying message that a working life containing no more than would-be authorship was fulfilling. And there would be something else: Ralph was publicity-conscious, and would be bound to renew his pleas that she join him and other members of the cast in seeking promotion via the media as a trailer to the series and a boost to their individual careers. Patrick had been disappointed that she had refused to take part in any publicity campaigns, but he had at least understood her refusal and accepted it. With her fellow players, Phyllida had had to cultivate the image of a loner – not a million miles from the truth – to explain her shrinking from publicity, and Ralph, because he was personally interested in her, was so far not accepting it.

To her relief, he seemed so grateful to have received an invitation that he began by allowing her to guide their conversation as well as their footsteps. It was a fine warm day and Seaminster was displaying itself with all its ephemeral charms in place, the sea blue-green and gently stirring under a clear blue sky, the sands washed clean by the night's high tide and colour-speckled with small colonies of the more sedate type of holidaymaker. Ralph had begun by wondering aloud how Phyllida could bury her fascinating self so far away from where things happened, but by the time they had strolled the curve of the bay he admitted that he half understood.

'And it's pretty accessible to London, of course. But you haven't been back. Unless you didn't let me know.'

'I haven't been back, but I have no sense of obligation to let you know if and when I do.' Phyllida said it with a smile, but her tone was clear: she wasn't joking.

Ralph gave a theatrical sigh and an out-sized shrug. He was handsome and he was nice, Phyllida admitted, with a pang of annoyance at her stubborn self-sufficiency.

But even if it wasn't in danger of being breached in another direction, she wouldn't link up with Ralph Harding. She had no need, she had long since discovered, of a lover without a special face.

But she enjoyed the day. They lunched in the open outside her favourite café, recalling the more amusing moments of the making of *A Policeman's Lot,* and it wasn't until the late afternoon, when Ralph had said he supposed it was time he made tracks and received no denial to his hopeful look, that he began to interrogate her on her refusal to join the publicity campaign.

'I know you like to do things on your own, worse luck for me, but this is just perverse. The campaign makes sense for everyone, Phyllida. You're intelligent, you must know it does!'

Phyllida looked into his exasperated face, the forehead ridged in bewilderment below at least a couple of inches of naturally up-standing dark hair, her mind trembling on the brink of explaining her exclusivity.

'I'm sorry, Ralph, it's just the way I am. Call it a weakness if you like, but I can't help it. I crawl at the mere thought of promoting myself.' It had been an effort to pull back, but Phyllida knew at once that she had done the right thing. 'And you know I'm not appearing in the credits under my own name. Joining the publicity campaign would make that difficult to maintain. I'm sorry.' She wasn't, really. Joining the campaign wouldn't have affected her as melo-dramatically as she had just proclaimed, but by temperament she was happier in her own persona out of the limelight. And if she wasn't asked to film again for TV she could live with it far more easily than she could live without the Peter Piper Detective Agency.

'So am I.' Ralph leaned forward and looked so hard into her eyes she had to force herself to hold his stare. 'I think you're hiding something,' he said at last. 'I think you don't want to be caught up with because of something in your past, that maybe you've already changed your name.'

He was still watching her carefully as she shrugged and smiled. 'Think that,' she said. 'It might make you less cross with me.'

'And it might have some truth in it.' They were sitting facing the sea, alone in a bay of one of the hyacinth-blue shelters, and Ralph got to his feet. 'I'll go back now, and you'll hope to goodness never to hear from me again.'

'That's certainly not true.' Phyllida rose too, and put a hand on his arm. 'I shall be sorry not to hear from you as my friend.'

'Perhaps you're a murderess,' he said. 'I could just about believe it.'

'No. I'm not that. Nor anything else sinister. Thank you for coming today, Ralph, I've enjoyed seeing you. And if I come up to London and it isn't a mad rush to get business done, I'll be in touch.'

He left her with a peck on the cheek, and a sense of regret and self-dissatisfaction that ebbed very slowly as Sunday's tide came in on another fine day.

Phyllida got up earlier than usual and dressed carefully – doing so for the first time in her own persona, she noted with wary amusement, since the days when she had wanted to please her husband. The red-haired Scotswoman who had attracted Dr Pusey had a natural clothes sense which Phyllida believed herself to lack, but at least they were both tall and slim and had good legs, and a sky-blue blouse on a finely pleated white skirt suited the day.

She arrived half an hour before the official proceedings, and spent it walking in the small gardens and sitting and anticipating with closed eyes turned to the sun. When she approached the old house which was the Gardens' administrative centre she found rows of seats facing a small platform erected on the lawn immediately in front of the main entrance. The seats were filling up, and a couple of young men and a young woman were standing beside the platform, shuffling the papers they were carrying and tensely smiling.

Phyllida was relieved to see that the centre of the front row was already taken, aware that she would have had an uncharacteristic struggle not to colonise it herself, but she sat down as near to it as she could. At ten o'clock, when the majority of the seats were occupied, one of the young men called for quiet, welcomed his audience, and, turning with an arm out towards the open doors of the house, announced the appearance of the Director.

Phyllida dropped her eyes to shield them from the coming dazzle, and when she raised them there was a man not much older than the first speaker standing in the front centre of the platform and saying what a splendid start it was to his directorship to preside at such a happy occasion.

At that point she lost sight and sound, and when they returned the man was concluding a short speech of welcome and telling his audience that he and his team would be available about the Gardens until four p.m., with an hour indoors from twelve thirty to one thirty, during which they would continue to answer visitors' questions over the buffet lunch.

'I think that's all I have to say now, except I would like to pay tribute to the outstanding contribution made over the past decade to the maintenance and development of these Gardens by my predecessor Dr Jack Pusey. Seaminster's loss is Edinburgh's gain, and I am well aware, ladies and gentlemen, of the quality of the act I have to follow.'

## Seven

Phyllida made her way quickly to the uncultivated outskirts of the Gardens, beyond where any of the experts had stationed themselves or were likely to appear. When there was no one to be seen in any direction she began to run, bawling at the blue indifference of the sky.

When she was exhausted she flung herself down on a patch of wild grasses and wept, and when she had no more tears she got to her feet and walked like a zombie to the gates and out to her car, hurt and insulted by the cheerful crowds.

She drove with particular care because she felt so unlike herself, and when she got home she ran immediately upstairs and threw herself across her bed.

It was afternoon when she sat up, blew her nose, and acknowledged her self-pity without any wish to escape it. There was no one else in the world at that moment, she railed at the walls, whose private life was more pitifully forlorn. And had been pitifully forlorn since adolescence, Phyllida angrily added, dragging out memories long and gladly buried. She had been the one to end all her relationships because they had never contained that special face. Until Gerald, but even then she had known in her heart that his was not the one. A small voice of reason tried to remind her that at least she had never loved and lost, but her self-pity countered with the angry retort that it was hardly less terrible never to have loved. And in a way she *had* loved Gerald, enough to be hurt by the affairs he had embarked on so soon after their marriage, and by his increasingly indifferent treatment of her.

Shuddering, Phyllida leapt off her bed and went downstairs and out into the garden, where she worked furiously until she was too tired to work any more. Then she went back indoors, poured herself a generous whisky, and rang the Agency.

The delay, and Peter's sleepy voice, gave her the answer before she had asked her question.

'Everything quiet, I gather.'

'Everything quiet. Is it as obvious as that?'

'Only to me, I'm sure.'

'Are you okay? You sound as if you've got a cold.'

'It's hay fever. Peter, all right if I don't wait till tomorrow to check out where our conspirators live?'

'All right for me if it's all right for you. It's *your* rest day.'

'I don't feel like resting.'

'Fine, then. You'll also discover which of their homes is going to be the easiest to park outside undetected.'

'I will.' She had heard his heavy sigh. 'You're all right?'

'Fine.' There was a pause. 'At a bit of a loose end.'

'Why don't you walk down to the sea? It's a lovely evening.' Horribly, mockingly lovely.

'Maybe I will.'

For a moment each thought of suggesting a meeting, but the energies of both of them were too self-absorbed, and the moment passed.

'Okay, then.'

'Okay.'

At least she appeared to be operating normally on a professional level, still curious to discover what sort of homes the leading lights of the Seaminster Theatre Company inhabited. Before leaving her own home Phyllida discovered from a combination of her local directory and a Seaminster street map that Amy Tate lived on the farther slopes of Great Hill, the large landmark at the east end of Seaminster's curve of bay, and Henry Hutton a couple of miles the other side of Little Hill, the smaller excrescence marking the west end of the bay, and her self-pity was for a moment breached by a mental picture of the two vanities crouched facing one another behind a rampart apiece of the town's two major geological features. The sight of Miss Bowden in her driving mirror was a further help, and made her thankful for once that

Phyllida Moon knew so few people in Seaminster. The odds were against someone recognising her car and wondering what an unknown woman in a very unflattering hat was doing at the wheel of it.

Geographically she was nearest to Henry Hutton, and decided to scout his area first.

Her street map of Seaminster led her away from the Parade soon after she had passed Little Hill, up a steep winding road which became steadily less maritime and more densely leafy as she climbed. The houses and their grounds grew as steadily larger, and on the crown of the ascent Henry Hutton's address appeared, consistent with Phyllida's reading of him: a large, red-brick, late Victorian house with lower floors well concealed behind the thick evergreen shrubbery of gothic literary convention. Phyllida could have believed from his demeanour that he was master of the whole imposing building, had the words 'The Laurels' in the telephone book not been qualified by the symbol '1'. Her heart sank as she looked from the house to the paper in her hand, and back again. From which section of the tall rambling building, and between which of the two sets of imposing gateposts, would Henry Hutton emerge?

The question was unanswerable without a reconnoitre, and maybe even with one, and Phyllida decided to check out the other addresses rather than get out of the car at that stage to investigate more closely. She could be forced to do so eventually, but she had to hope now that the point of departure from the homes of her other suspects would be less ambiguous.

Amy Tate's was alarmingly so. The other side of town from Phyllida's semi, it could have been the product of the same inter-war builder, but it lacked Phyllida's containing sandstone wall and screening front bushes, presenting a naked air to passers-by and reciprocally laying them open to full scrutiny from Miss Tate's upper and lower front bay windows.

Barely slowing down, Phyllida continued along the road – another, slighter, upward incline which ended in a T-junction – and turned right towards the address the local phone book offered for its only Swain, C. Phyllida had no evidence that Carol lived alone, but her reading of the girl made her hopeful of being on the way to where she lived.

Number Twenty-One Hillside Crescent was, as its name suggested, on yet another incline, this one a slight downward slope on the way back to the sea about half a mile beyond Miss Tate's and just into the ongoing bungaloid development that was doing its best to bridge the distance between Seaminster and the much smaller resort of Billingon-Sea. It was less open to the road than Miss Tate's house, but this road too was narrow and a waiting car would stand out.

There was no evidence of Ben Carson's involvement in – or even knowledge of – the event which was to take place for Amy Tate, Henry Hutton and Carol Swain in three days' time, but Carol was his girlfriend, and it had been obvious on Phyllida's last visit to the theatre green-room that he had been anxious to keep Miss Tate silent on the subject of other interest groups. After looking him up in both her guide books she set off hopefully back into town, buoying herself up with the thought that of the Little Theatre people she had so far met Ben Carson was the closest to her subject. And, in the town setting of both his home and his place of work, he might also be closest to an unobtrusive parking place.

'Paul! Why are you here?'

Ben Carson's question came gently but quickly the moment the gallery door had closed on the client to whom he had just sold a picture, and Paul Harper, skulking in a corner and looking down at the foot he was scuffing on the edge of the thick grey carpet rather than at anything on the walls, came as quickly to attention.

'Because I wanted to see you,' he retorted pettishly, advancing to the reception counter behind which his friend was standing. 'That's a crime, is it?'

'Don't be silly. But you're obviously in a mood, which isn't a good time to visit me here. Especially as we'll be meeting tomorrow at the theatre, where a show of temperament is marginally more appropriate.'

'I'm not in a mood, Ben. I'm just...' The pettishness had gone and the boy's face was suddenly despairing.

'Just what?' Ben enquired resignedly, pointing to the chair Paul's side of the counter as he himself sat down.

Paul threw himself into it. 'When are we going to come clean?' he asked despairingly. 'It gets harder and harder.'

'I know.'

'Can't you talk to Carol?'

'I've told you I can. When I judge the time's right.'

The sudden sternness in Carson's tone made Paul recoil blinking, but within seconds he had rallied. 'Can't you give me some idea of when that'll be?'

'Soon. It'll be soon. But don't push me.'

Paul threw his arms out in a gesture of helplessness. 'Sorry, sorry. It's just ... I'm scared. Of myself. Of – everything. Mum and Dad know there's something up, they've starting questioning me about where I'm going, when I'll be back, and so on. They're thinking about Hugh's arrest, Ben, they're afraid–'

'Then for God's sake try to behave normally. Force yourself to smile, appear lighthearted. The standard schoolboy son. If this is as important to you as you tell me it is, you should be able to cope. Unless you want them to find out?' There was a visible tension in Ben Carson as he waited for the answer to his question.

'God, no.'

'Very well, then.' The dark eyes softened. 'You have to accept that you can't have it both ways. Neither can I, and that's my problem.' The bitter little laugh made Paul Harper wince. 'You've got to understand,

Paul, how much more difficult things are for me, how carefully they have to be handled. Now, you'd better go. There'll be a chance to talk at the theatre tomorrow.'

'Can't I come round to your place tonight?'

'No. I'm sorry. Carol and I are invited out to dinner. Now, go home and be patient and *work*. I don't want you to worry about your A levels the way you're making out in public that you're worrying, but they really are important. And you've got the brains to do well; it'll be a wicked waste if you don't.'

'I know. It's just that – the ninth. I hoped that before the ninth–'

'The ninth makes no difference. But if you don't feel you can cope with it, you'd better stay away.'

'No! I want to be there. My first time ... I'll be all right. And I won't come to the gallery again unless you invite me.'

'You can come to the gallery any time you like as a friend who's wondering if I've any interesting new pictures. Not to try and talk – business.' Ben Carson's eyes travelled the extent of his small space. 'It's just as well there's no one here today.'

There was in fact a woman. Absorbed, catalogue in hand, in one of the more conventional of his pictures. But a glance at her dreary insignificance had assured Ben Carson that she was as harmless as the space surrounding her.

'So Mary Bowden passed her first real test with flying colours,' Phyllida finished, without feeling immodest. But she wasn't talking about herself. 'It took me all my time not to smile, the airy way Carson dismissed her.'

Suspecting that her boss as well as herself could earlier in the day have been nursing a delicate ego, Phyllida had for the first time telephoned the office in the late evening to gauge his mood instead of presenting herself in the Square and reading his window code. She had had no intention of attempting to see him that Sunday night, but following the small supper she had forced herself to prepare and to eat she had felt so depressed by the prospect of her own unhappy company through to the following morning that she had found herself reaching for the telephone.

That she wasn't going in person, she realised ruefully as she listened to the heartless ringing tone, was probably as much because she dreaded the message of Peter's dark windows as because she didn't want to intrude on someone else's malaise.

She was just about to hang up when the ringing tone cut out and Peter's sleepy voice offered a grumpy, 'Yes?'

'It's Phyllida. I'm sorry, I know it's Sunday and I'm not at the Golden Lion, but I've had an interesting evening workwise and I just thought you might–'

'Gosh, yes!' She heard the instant transformation, and thought wearily of how much easier it always seemed to be for men. 'Were you just thinking of telling me on the phone, or could you possibly consider–'

'I'd consider presenting myself for a drink.'

'You would? That's wonderful! How soon can you make it?'

'I'm almost ready. I'll be with you in twenty minutes.'

Phyllida was ready then, and in the car she could have reached the Agency in less than half that time. But before telephoning she had gone to lean on her front garden gate and look out over the sea. The moon was low on the horizon beneath a clear sky thick with stars, and the silver-gilt path it was casting to the near-motionless water's edge seemed to beckon her to set foot on it. She had decided then that the next best thing would be to walk along beside it, prolonging the tantalising challenge and savouring the warm dark air of a perfect summer night. She would do it even if Peter didn't answer her call, or made it clear that he didn't want to see her, and then possibly she might sleep, and wake up nearer the more comfortable self she had grown accustomed to living with during the past seaside year.

Her walk – with the black bulk of Great Hill rearing against the navy-blue, star-studded sky ahead of her, and the mocking challenge of the watery walkway keeping pace with her the length of the Parade – was so headily lovely that by the time she arrived at the Agency she was recovered enough to be looking forward to the customary drink and chat.

Her first Scotch was waiting on the desk in front of her chair, and Peter had left the window from which he had saluted her as she crossed the Square and was sitting down and looking expectant.

'What did you make of the Harper-Carson exchange?' he asked her with interest when he had heard her report.

'I'm not sure. I've a feeling there was something in it I couldn't read. Carson's a controlled sort of chap, but he gave me the impression he's just as unhappy in his way as Paul Harper. At least I learned that Harper and Carson as well as Carol Swain are in on the Hutton-Tate conspiracy. And it confirms the importance of the ninth.'

'Still no clue as to a.m. or p.m.?'

'None,' Phyllida said regretfully. 'I keep thinking someone's said something about it being the night, then I realise that's just my own idea because it sounds more conspiratorial.'

'So surveillance will have to start in the early morning. I think we must all be in position by seven a.m. And I'm afraid to say I think we should carry on all day even if we discover that our subjects aren't going to do anything significant at eleven thirty a.m., in case eleven thirty p.m. is an away date. We'll break the bad news to Steve in the morning.' Peter studied Phyllida's face anxiously, the anxiety fading as it showed neither surprise nor dismay. 'You'd realised it already, hadn't you?'

Phyllida nodded, smiling. 'You're talking about "we"?'

'Yep. Now we know Harper and Carson are involved I've decided the ninth needs the three of us.' The excitement that made

Phyllida see him as a schoolboy was sparkling in Peter's eyes as he looked at her over the rim of his glass before setting it down, springing to his feet and striding over to his nearer window, where he stood looking out. 'I think Swain's the one to leave out,' he said, turning round after a few moment's silent contemplation of the glittering night sky. 'Carson may be giving her a lift – maybe Harper, too. And from what you've told me, his will be the easiest address to keep under observation. Can you tell me more about his home and workplace set-up?' Peter left the window to reach for her glass, which he refilled along with his own before throwing himself back in his chair and fixing her with a look of eager anticipation.

'His flat's just along the road from his gallery, which means it's in a stretch of busy street. It's actually over an estate agent's, with a slim front door between the agent's and the next door premises, which is a shoe shop. One storey and a couple of good-sized windows with clean net curtains. I didn't see any signs for restricted parking, but I'll be surprised if it isn't. I didn't see any for residents' spaces either, but that's probably because the street's predominantly commercial. There are bound to be cars parked all night, though, and there could be a problem finding a space. But if we can slot into one we should be just about invisible. And whoever takes Carson on will be able to watch him going to work without getting out of the car.'

'And if he doesn't go to work, you'll follow him. I'd like Mary Bowden to take Carson, Phyllida. All right?'

'Yes!'

'Mrs Sheridan didn't get any clue as to where he keeps his car, if he has one? Good God, how could she have done?' Peter answered his question immediately with a second, rhetorical one, looking apologetic. 'It's because I know you're a witch that I think of these impossible things.'

'When Sonia Sheridan was collecting curricula vitae round the table in the Little Theatre she or Carson could have said something about the difficulty of knowing what to do with your car when you live in the centre of town, but I'm afraid neither of them did. I'll get another chance during the coffee and biscuits that's bound to follow the casting tomorrow night. I'll find out then, too, whether Miss Tate and Henry Hutton have cars.'

'I'm sure you will.'

'Your and Steve's problems will be just the opposite. You'll have your roadways to yourselves. Will you take Tate or Hutton?'

'I'll leave Hutton to Steve; he can do a preliminary recce after dark tomorrow. He's a chameleon when he's on the prowl, I saw him once. He'll sort out Hutton's exit point.'

'And Hutton's road is wide and leafy, so Steve won't be anything like as conspicuous as you will outside Amy Tate's bald semi. But you look so responsible and respectable you'll charm her into submission if she gets suspicious and taps on your window.'

'Let's hope so. But I shan't be that close, although I'll park on her side of the road – she'll be less aware of me there if she looks up and down before taking off wherever it is she's clandestinely going. Thanks again, Phyllida.'

Phyllida recognised the last three words as Peter's usual polite form of dismissal, and got to her feet. 'Are you going home to-night?'

Peter stood up too, shaking his head. 'Thought I'd stay here. I had a drink before you came. Will you be all right? Your room's always there at the Golden Lion.'

'I know, but I ate enough before I came out. I'll be OK.' She wouldn't tell him she hadn't got the car, present him unnecessarily with the dilemma of deciding between safety and gallantry. And she was looking forward to another walk.

Peter was at his window when she crossed the Square, and they both waved as she entered the narrow passageway beside the Golden Lion, the most direct way to both its car park and the Parade.

Moon and stars were as brilliant as they had been when she left home, the stars as highly remote, the moon as apparently accessible with its path to the shore still beckoning her. The only changes were the drop in temperature which brought a crisp tap of air to her cheeks and forehead, and the slight lift of her spirits.

## Eight

The element of luck which Peter firmly believed to be present somewhere in every case – so long as the investigator was doing everything humanly possible without it – came to Phyllida's aid the moment she entered the Little Theatre's rehearsal room the following night. She found Amy Tate and Ben Carson in the midst of a small, irritable group comparing their experiences of the traffic standstill that had afflicted the town centre during the early evening's slight increase in road usage which the inhabitants of Seaminster called the rush hour.

Miss Tate greeted Mrs Sheridan effusively, bringing Clive Simpson's account of his experience to a premature end, and enquired if she had been a victim. Phyllida had been ready for a car-related question from her first visit to the Little Theatre, and Mrs Sheridan informed the group that she was without one in Seaminster, hinting at the last stages of convalescence from un-specified surgery which temporarily forbade driving but encouraged walking. 'Which is such a pleasure in this delightful little town.' Fortunately Miss Tate had not yet made her contribution to the traffic hold-up stories, and let Mrs Sheridan's information and compliment pass with no more than a reflex smirk.

'I was stationary for a quarter of an hour!' she complained. 'But at least I switched off my engine. The man in front of me just sat there belching out filth until I knocked on his window and suggested it was time he started thinking about the environment!'

'And what was his reaction?' Ben Carson's expression was a mixture of curiosity and alarm.

'What do you think? He told me to ... Well, you can guess.' Miss Tate's shudder briefly revealed her bodily excrescences as her inadequately tented dress resettled over them. 'But when I'd been back in my car for five minutes the noxious fumes stopped coming so I must have made him think.' Henry Hutton had strolled up, and she turned to him. 'Did you have any trouble driving in town this evening, Henry? With that great vehicle of yours.'

'My great vehicle was not in town this evening, Amy. Nor any other. When I need to make a journey as short as a visit to town I walk, or take a bus or a taxi. If more people did that there would be no problem.' Phyllida was so aware of the point scoring between Hutton and Miss Tate she could see them with her mind's eye alternately raising an index finger to mark a one-up on the air. As she could also see Hutton at the wheel of some stately veteran that yielded him some nine or ten miles per gallon.

'It was a burst water main, Henry,' Ben Carson said, as, each raising eyebrows in deadpan faces, Hutton and Simpson turned away without further comment and started to mount the stage.

'It's the sort of thing that makes Ben smug,' Carol Swain contributed. 'Seeing it takes him about a dozen steps to get from home to work and back.'

'But isn't the down side of that having difficulty finding a parking space?' Mrs Sheridan enquired. The point had arrived where the luck would run out if Phyllida didn't help it along.

Carson nodded. 'And because I live in a commercial area there are no reserved spaces for residents.'

'And restricted daytime parking, I guess?' Mrs Sheridan suggested, Phyllida's fingers crossed against her cream silk skirt.

'No, although the city fathers have started talking about it. The yellow line's broken on one side of Horton Street, so if I manage to get in I'm all right. If I'm unlucky I tend to end up in the small car park off Moss Street, but I can't always find a place even in there during the tourist season. Like now. But at least that doesn't make me late for work.'

'But you're surely able to slot into your own street late at night or in the early morning?' Sonia Sheridan's drawl hid Phyllida's pang of alarm.

'If I get there soon after six in the evening I can probably manage it. But I'm unlikely to be looking for a place then as I'm usually still in the Gallery. I've noticed a few spaces between, say, six and eight in the morning, when the overnighters have started leaving and the day people are only beginning to arrive. So if I could be bothered I could always bring–'

'Do you think we might start talking about the play?'

Henry Hutton's soft, weary voice had a surprisingly strong carrying quality that made Phyllida wonder if he had trained for the professional stage, and the group obediently broke up into a dozen or so people taking their places in the rows of chairs drawn up in front of the stage. Encouraged by their example, another small group standing hesitantly in the doorway followed suit. Phyllida was pleased to see June Jones among these, but she appeared not to notice Mrs Sheridan's nod and smile and sat down some places away.

After a few fussy moments Amy, Henry, Carol, Ben and Clive Simpson were the only people on their feet, and Hutton offered Miss Tate an ironic bow and an indication that she should precede him up the steps to the stage, where again there was a short row of chairs.

Carol and Clive brought up the rear and immediately sat down, but Miss Tate made no move until Hutton's rigidly upright stance and the fixity of his gaze in her direction appeared finally to defeat her and with a grimly mutinous smile she gave in and collapsed ungracefully on to the chair next to Carol's. Hutton then turned his attention to the waiting audience.

It was his moment. He spoke, Phyllida reckoned, for ten or fifteen minutes, talking about playwriting in general, his own new play, and how vital it was that it should be correctly cast.

'You see,' he told them, 'this play has rather more substance than the plays I have written for you hitherto. In the first place, I wrote it for myself. It has something to say.' Henry fixed his eyes on a point well beyond his audience – as if, Phyllida fancied, envisaging one far larger – and held his long gaze for several seconds, coming back to sparse reality with a regretful sigh.

'On a practical level,' he resumed, 'it also has quite a large cast, with some crowd scenes, so we shall be able to involve more of you than is usually possible.' Amy, who had struggled up into a more dignified position on her narrow chair, nodded encouragingly to the groundlings, from whom there came a gratified murmur.

'Now.' Henry glanced along the chairs on the platform, as if to signal the end of his solo act, and the four people beside him, led by Miss Tate, responded with smiles and slight movements indicating their readiness to play their parts in the imminent casting process. 'The five of us up here,' Henry went on, 'will be better able to assess your efforts at a slight distance. Conventionally of course we should reverse our positions, but we have found that our would-be players tend to be more relaxed and uninhibited if allowed to read from among the audience.' Another approving murmur. 'Good. Now,' Henry repeated, looking for the first time less than totally in control, and Phyllida correctly anticipated the reason a second before his glance narrowed down on to her. 'There are a couple of parts for which I am fairly confident – subject, of course, to the agreement of my fellow judges–' Phyllida suspected irony again, although Miss Tate obviously took his reference at face value as she made a satisfied nestling movement that caused her chair to sway – 'that there are obvious castings. One is the mysterious mature lady with the mid-Atlantic accent.' Hutton nodded towards Mrs Sheridan, and Phyllida, thankful to be out of sight inside her cocoon, was aware of her fellow aspirants turning to look at her. 'I trust Mrs Sheridan will not think I am decrying her delightful voice when I use that phrase. I am not referring to the obnoxious habit of London *disc jockeys*–' the disdainful stress made the appellation sound like an obscenity – 'of disguising their vocal origins with what they imagine to be an American accent. I am talking about theatrical ambiguity, and the mere hint of the New World which is all Mrs Sheridan brought to her rendition of the Countess Olivia the other memorable night. It will perfectly reflect the equivocal character of my Mrs Castlereagh...'

'I was terribly afraid we were in for a dose of sub-Wilde,' Phyllida told Peter three hours later. 'But what I've seen of the play so far, it's quite original and really rather good. Hutton's a clever old bird as well as a downy one. And as cold as a fish.'

In view of her forced admission of her lack

of a car, Phyllida had received more than one invitation to be driven back to the Golden Lion. Although it was another fine night and she would have relished the walk, she accepted Carol Swain's offer in the line of duty, and made no immediate move to get out of the girl's small red Renault when it had stopped at the hotel.

'That was a very gratifying evening,' she said with a smile, as she and Carol turned to look at one another. 'I really don't deserve such star treatment.'

'You're different,' Carol said, smiling back. 'You're something new for us. I suppose we'll lose you, though, if you don't live in Seaminster. Unless you're thinking of buying a property here?' she added hopefully.

Phyllida shook her head. 'I don't know, Carol, I really don't. I like Seaminster so very much, I've really fallen for its charms. But I'm a restless soul. I don't have roots these days and I tend to move around.'

'Part of me would like to be like that,' Carol said in a rush, and Phyllida suspected her of making the rare confession which can be easier to make to a stranger than to somebody known. 'But the main part ... I'm ambitious. And I'll stick like glue to whatever'll get me where I want to be. Making oneself independent is the thing, isn't it?'

'From Ben?'

Mrs Sheridan asked the question lightly and teasingly, while Phyllida watched keenly for Carol's response.

It was not what she expected. The single-minded, slightly hard look in the girl's bright blue eyes faltered and her strong mouth softened, making Phyllida aware for the first time of the attractively defined fullness of her lips. 'They say there's always an exception to prove the rule, don't they?' Carol said, with a sudden grin. 'Yes, I'm a softie where Ben's concerned.'

'And he's clearly a softie where you're concerned, too.' It was a question rather than a statement: neither Carol nor Ben was the type to show their feelings for one another in public, and Phyllida had learned little or nothing about their relationship.

Carol's face lit up. 'Yes. He is. We're both terribly lucky.'

'I'm so glad, honey. When do you plan to be married?'

'Oh, I don't know, we're like an old married couple now who happen to own two homes. I think we'll just turn to one another one day and say let's go and do it and slide off with a couple of close friends to a registry office. Then maybe have a party to celebrate.' Carol clasped her knees and smiled contentedly through the windscreen.

'You know, I like that idea.' So did Phyllida. 'Now, what was up with your young friend Paul this evening? He missed the casting and I didn't think he looked too bright when he arrived for the coffee.'

'I don't think he is.' Concern came into Carol's face, but not enough to dislodge the evidence of her own sense of well being.

'Still exams?'

'I expect so. He's rather highly strung.'

'Ben seems to handle him well.'

Carol smiled. 'I know. Some people think Ben's surly, but he's just reserved. He's terribly kind and understanding.'

'I'm sure. Now, I mustn't keep you any longer but I've just had a thought.' A mischievous one that Phyllida wished had occurred to her while she was around Amy Tate. 'What about coming to have a drink with me at the hotel on Wednesday evening? With Ben, of course.'

'Wednesday...' What Phyllida had been testing was Carol's skill at dissembling, and she had to give it full marks. There had been no overreaction, and the pause for thought would have seemed genuine to anyone not knowing the girl had a vital prior engagement. 'Wednesday,' Carol repeated. 'No, I'm afraid I'm already booked for Wednesday. But I should love to come another night.'

'Good. We'll arrange it soon. Good-night, Carol.' Mrs Sheridan climbed elegantly out of the car, and Phyllida saw with relief that Peter's light was on and that he was standing at his window. She had never been more eager to sort out her reactions aloud.

'They're tied up on Wednesday evening,' she told him a few minutes later. 'But I don't suppose we dare assume that that rules out eleven thirty a.m. They could have an all-day appointment.'

'They could. But it was a good try.'

'It told me Carol Swain will never give anything away.'

'You've just said she gave away the fact that Carson's her Achilles heel.'

'Because she sees that as one of her strengths. "Out of the strong came forth sweetness." It makes her happier with her self-image.'

'You're quite the philosopher tonight.'

'Sorry. I suppose I'm feeling above myself. Elated with all the lionising.' It was a dangerous elation, she knew that; the desperate flip side of the desolation that had engulfed her with the knowledge that Jack Pusey had gone away. It would, of course, collapse like a bubble when she reminded herself that it had nothing to do with Phyllida Moon. But like St Augustine and his chastity, for once in her life she would try for a while to postpone that reminder. 'Now, I've a few more things to tell you.'

'Fire away.' Peter leaned down to his disguised drinks cabinet and brought out bottles and glasses. 'Were you able to pick anything up out of the rush hour chaos?'

'Yes! They were all going on about it when I arrived and I got what we needed on a plate. Our three principals all drive, though Henry's more likely to take a bus or a taxi for short journeys. Carol drove me back to the hotel and gave me a chance to get Carson's registration number, since they were parked side by side in the Little Theatre park. Which is going to be useful, as I also found out the problems carwise of living and working in Horton Street. The best news of the evening was that there's unrestricted parking on one side, which means that once I've got a space I can hold on to it until Carson moves. He said there's a chance of finding a space before eight a.m., when the night people are starting to give way to the day. I rather think that if Carson doesn't emerge from his gallery in the morning I'd be wise to leave my car there until he does. Not my car, of course, Peter,' Phyllida added anxiously.

'Of course not your car. I've a tame car hire firm, from which I've already arranged for Miss Bowden to collect a Ford Fiesta at three p.m. tomorrow. A Mr Jarvis will attend to her.'

'Thanks.' Phyllida grinned her relief. 'I should have known.' She knew that Peter had a collection of what he called his tame contacts, including a detective sergeant in the local force, on whom he seemed able to call with confidence as specific needs arose.

'You can take it straight to the Golden Lion car park. It might also be a good idea...' Peter paused, and Phyllida completed what she knew he was wanting to say.

'To stay the night at the hotel. Of course.'

'I shouldn't get to Horton Street too early, you want to be as inconspicuous as possible. Say seven to seven thirty.'

'Right. I'll start cruising earlier though, to find Carson's car. If I find it easily I can always sit in the Moss Street car park for a while. That's where it might be anyway, he told Mrs Sheridan he sometimes ends up there.'

'Mrs Sheridan certainly encourages people to talk.'

'Because she's such an entirely different species, I suspect. So distant she's entirely unthreatening. Carol was a surprise, though. I didn't expect Mrs S to do as well with her as she did.'

'Any more?'

Peter refilled the glasses and settled back. By the time she had told him the rest of her gleanings, Phyllida had decided to spend that night at the Golden Lion, too. She would have to go to her room there anyway to dispose of Sonia Sheridan, and the replication of her basic needs – clothes, cosmetics – made it possible to decide to stay overnight without any special preparation.

'This June Jones,' Peter said, 'was she offered a role without reading for it?'

'Yes. The only other person besides Mrs Sheridan. A character as ambiguous as Mrs Castlereagh's accent. I have to say both Hutton and Miss Tate seem to know what they're doing. Miss Jones is to play one of those characters one scarcely notices who watch and listen and act on what they pick up. So devastatingly in this character's case,

Henry told us, that she's the catalyst for the denouement. Which we don't know yet; he's keeping us in suspense till the next time, we were only given act one.'

'Was it – all right?'

'Of course. I enjoyed it.'

'You didn't feel – demeaned?'

'Of course not,' Phyllida said, laughing. 'It's part of my job. My main job.' Feeling as she did in a whirl of uncertainties, it seemed the time to get one thing straight. 'Working for the Agency is more important to me now than any straight acting job.'

'Any acting job for TV?'

'Any acting job at all.'

'So you'd feel pretty bad if I didn't agree to take you back after your next summons?'

'I feel bad now that you've asked me that.' Angry, rather than upset.

'I'm sorry, I'm sorry!' Peter leaned imploringly across his desk. 'I'm just conjuring up the worst case scenario because I'm such a miserable pessimist I have to prod at any luck that comes my way, it's so hard for me to accept it. It's what the ancients called 'accidia'. An inability to accept good fortune.'

'Oh, Peter! We're more alike than I'd imagined.'

'Not you, too?'

'I'm afraid so. I've sometimes suspected I have the power to turn the postman away from the gate.'

'I know what you mean. We'll have to fight it together. Of course I'll have you back after your next summons. And I'm over the moon, Miss Moon, that you see this as your number one job. I'll stop picking at it. Thanks.'

'Thank you, Peter.' Phyllida got to her feet, ashamed at last of her self-pity. She knew, though, that the bleakness was still waiting to pounce and was glad to be spending the night in her impersonal office room, where she would be protected from its full effect by the sense of being at work which she never quite shed when she was at the Golden Lion, even in her sleep.

## Nine

'The chief thing to remember,' Peter said, 'is that if and when we tail our respective subjects to what we deem to be the rendez-vous we *drive past*. Without any slowing down unless there's some obstruction. And we don't stop or use our mobiles until we're sure we're out of sight. Not that we should need to do either unless there's some serious hitch. If there isn't, Steve and I will keep going and leave the field to Phyllida, who will backtrack to the rendezvous on foot. All right?'

Steve and Phyllida both nodded, but Phyllida noted the ebbing of the colour in Steve's normally pale face that always appeared at the prospect of action which accorded with the Boys' Own concept of private detective work she knew he still cherished.

'That's if our quest turns out to be local,' Peter went on, getting up from his desk and going across to his window, where he stood looking out. Phyllida was aware of Steve twitching in his chair as she watched a newly sprung west wind drive sculpted white cloud across a hard blue sky. 'If it ends at the station Phyllida will abandon her car – in the station park if possible – and travel with the subjects. And if they drive out of town we'll all keep after them until they reach their destination, when Steve and I will drive off, as we'll do locally, once we're satisfied Phyllida can cope. All right, Steve?'

Peter had turned with unexpected speed from the window, in time to catch the discontent in Steve's face.

'Don't you think a man–' Steve began passionately, but Peter cut him short.

'You're a super sleuth, Steve, but Phyllida's the only one of us who'll be in disguise, who can take the risk of being seen. And this is her case. We wouldn't be making plans now if it wasn't for all the things she's managed to find out. Things we couldn't have discovered without her special skills. And I'm confident she can cope. Am I right, Phyllida?'

'I'm expecting to cope,' Phyllida told him.

Peter nodded, satisfied. 'That's the most any of us can truthfully say. Does either of you have any questions?'

Steve shrugged. 'I could bring Melanie on board. If I do have to stop for any reason – another traffic hold-up, say – nobody'll think of worrying about me if I'm groping my passenger.'

'Only the police if your eyes are off the road,' Peter said sternly. 'But it's not a bad idea.'

'What about Melanie's real job?' Phyllida asked. During her time at the Agency she had developed a concerned sympathy for the skinny compliant girlfriend Steve appeared to pick up and put down as it pleased him.

'She'll phone in sick,' Steve said complacently, and Phyllida believed him: poor Melanie was unlikely to pass up on the rare opportunity of a day alone with her beloved in a confined space.

'I don't want to know about that,' Peter said. 'But I'm happy for you to bring her along if she's willing and able to come. Anything else? No? Then take the rest of the day off, both of you, keeping your phone lines open.' Peter glanced from his wall clock to Phyllida. 'Miss Bowden's car should be ready for collection in an hour, so you'll be wanting to conjure her up.'

Phyllida paused in Reception, to try and cajole Jenny out of her sense of being the one to miss out. 'We couldn't do it if you weren't here to keep things going. Detectives are two-a-penny compared with secretaries-cum-bookkeepers-cum-office managers. Truly, Jenny. Now, I've got to go and turn into Miss Bowden so that I can collect her car. But I'm just wondering...' Phyllida's own car was behind the Golden Lion, and she had reluctantly decided to go home in it when she had parked the hire car there and shed Mary Bowden. A few hours' gardening and some work on her book would help pass the time – she anticipated a queasy mixture of personal depression and professional excitement – until she could get back to work by moving into her hotel room. Anything that hastened that return would be welcome. 'How about coming over to the Golden Lion when you finish here for the day, Jenny, and having an early supper with me? I'd welcome your company; it would stop me thinking too much about tomorrow. It'll be prudent, I'm afraid, to eat upstairs, but you won't mind that?'

Jenny grinned, transformed. 'As if! It'd be fab to have supper with you, Phyllida. Thanks a million.'

'I'll tell Reception I'm expecting you and they'll direct you to my room.'

'Which I've never seen!'

In the event Jenny didn't see it until she was leaving, and then for no more than a moment, because the hotel management decided to set their supper out in a vacant suite on the posh side of the door that divided the more thickly-piled corridor carpets from the thinner. The gesture warmed Phyllida out of the chill she had brought back with her from home and she was almost able to enjoy Jenny's talkative company – the main subject of conversation being Kevin Keithley and Jenny's anxious hope that he had no part in the secret meeting – and feel ready to sleep when she had told Jenny it was time to go. Glad, even, that she and Peter had decided not to meet in the office that night.

To her grateful surprise, lying down and sitting up to switch off her alarm felt like one continuous movement, and from the moment of waking there was no time for personal thoughts. The out-of-the-office Mary Bowden was not a complex creature and Phyllida hoped she would spend the day in virtual isolation, but as with all her characters she must harness her mind in the making of her, and the set of Miss Bowden's mouth as she took her final look in the mirror was as important as the pallor of her skin and the harsh lines of her hair.

Phyllida emerged through the back door of the hotel into a dazzle of pale sun that had just cleared the serrated summits of the Parade buildings to the east of the bay. The air was already warm and it looked as if the day's weather would be as fine as Miss Tate's forecast had promised. Phyllida drove straight to Horton Street where, as Ben

Carson had predicted, there were a few available parking spaces. But it was only half-past six and, mindful of Peter's injunction, she drove reluctantly past them, needing all her willpower not to slot into one when she saw Ben Carson's car almost directly opposite the Gallery. Half an hour in the Moss Street park seemed like a very long time, even with the distraction of leaving the car to visit a newsagent for a morning paper and doing the crossword, and it was almost as much of a relief to be on the move again as to find the ideal space – a little way short of both Carson's home and his Gallery – still available. Phyllida decided she would look less furtive facing the two premises than peering between her rear and wing mirrors, and it was certainly more comfortable. So much so that within a quarter of an hour of parking she awoke from a doze. Her watch told her she had lost only two minutes but it was a warning, and an indication of how long the day might be.

Peter had a disgruntled call from Steve as he followed Amy Tate into the car park of an out-of-town supermarket just after twelve noon.

'Hutton hasn't budged. There's nothing

round here but big gardens, so I've had to go in his bushes. Melanie's crossing her legs.'

'So send her into the bushes too; according to Phyllida they're dense enough to protect her modesty. Phyllida's static as well; Carson's in his gallery. I'm in Sainsbury's car park and about to go shopping with Miss Tate. You can still ring me, but keep it for when Hutton makes a move.'

As he prowled the aisles, selecting various items of shopping he really needed, Peter decided that a supermarket was a comparatively easy place in which to carry out surveillance. Every shopper was so intent on the shelves that even when greeted by friends or acquaintances they took a few moments to come to and refocus their eyes. Miss Tate spent a deeply absorbed half hour making her selections, then wheeled her packed trolley into the coffee shop, where she parked it in a designated slot and joined the short queue for food. Peter allowed three other people to follow her before joining the queue himself and selecting a cheese and pickle sandwich and a cup of black coffee. When he looked up from the till Miss Tate was settling herself at a table in the window. There was a vacant one next to it, where he sat down facing her back.

At first he put her anxiety down to her enforced wait for the all-day breakfast which she weighed into with gusto the moment it arrived. But she still wasn't relaxed, and was looking every few moments towards the entrance, so it was a confirmation of Peter's hopes rather than a surprise when another woman of her age and almost her build came puffing across the room and flopped down in the chair facing him.

'Amy! So sorry I'm late! It's just that–'

'You're always late,' Miss Tate responded amiably. 'Not to worry. You'd better go and get some food. The brunch is excellent.'

'Oh, I haven't got that sort of appetite.' Perhaps a slight retaliation. 'Not *today*.'

There was a tingling along Peter's spine as he blessed a pair of ears that picked up nuances.

'Whatever you decide to eat, Matty, you have to fetch it.'

'Yes. I'll get a sandwich and some coffee. Shan't be a jiffy.'

Alone again, Miss Tate returned to her brunch with full concentration, and she was putting her knife and fork together on an empty plate as her friend returned with the equivalent of Peter's selection.

'Have you shopped?' Miss Tate enquired, after a deep draught of tea.

'Oh... No, I'll pick up a few things afterwards. I'm too excited to concentrate properly.'

'Try to keep a sense of proportion, Matty. It's only... Well, you know what it is. Freedom and Joy.'

Peter heard the capital letters, and knew Miss Tate was quoting a slogan. One that slightly checked his excitement until he managed to persuade himself that it could make psychological sense for drug users to attempt to elevate their activity by giving it a vaguely uplifting title. Especially if they were like Miss Tate and her friend. And whatever it turned out to be, there was certainly *something* afoot that was not to be spoken about openly.

'Yes, I'm ready, Amy, but I was just wondering...'

Speculation could come later. Peter switched back hastily into listening mode.

'What?'

'To help me pinpoint... Which is the nearest road down to that stretch of beach? The Parade peters out at Red Rocks, and I think it has to be a mile or two beyond. Last time you took me–'

'Oh, all right, Matty.' Amy Tate gave a gusty sigh and pushed her chair back so vigorously it struck the facing chair at Peter's table and made his cutlery rattle. Her companion cast a brief anxious glance towards him, but Miss Tate failed to turn round. 'You're making such heavy weather of it I'd better take you again. The fewer cars around the better anyway, I suppose. Be looking out for me at eleven fifteen sharp.'

'Oh, thank you, Amy! I wasn't asking – but I'm very grateful. And I'm not all that good these days driving at night.'

'Right. Well.' Miss Tate heaved herself to her feet, and Peter picked up his mug of coffee to prevent a spill. 'I'll see you tonight, Matty.'

'It's very good of you, Amy. How many are we expecting?'

'Pretty well the full complement.'

'Ah, yes. The time of year—'

'It shouldn't make any difference,' Miss Tate responded severely.

'I suppose not.'

'Goodbye, Matty.' Threading her way was not an appropriate metaphor for Miss Tate, but it occurred to Peter as he watched her swift negotiation of people and tables without any apparent collision on her way to retrieving her trolley and pushing it vigorously out of sight. He finished his coffee and followed her, after seeing her friend lean back with a contented sigh and what he read with growing bewilderment as an anticipatory smile.

'Oh, Steve... You don't have to stop just 'cos there's no one passing.'

'I'm ready for a sandwich. And a drink.' Steve disengaged himself from Melanie and reached down for the plastic box and the Thermos. 'Aren't you?'

'Could be, I suppose.' Melanie hitched her sleeveless top back into place with a twitch of her thin shoulders.

'Come on, then.'

Steve's mobile rang just as he took his first bite, and, anticipating his boss, he chewed and swallowed rapidly before responding.

'Steve!' It was Phyllida.

'Yes?' Steve enquired thickly, having vented his disappointment on a second, and larger, mouthful of cheese and pickle.

'You're having lunch. All right, you only have to listen. Peter's struck lucky, he's found out that the rendezvous is tonight on or near a stretch of beach a mile or two past Red Rocks. That's all we know, but it's a lot and it takes the sweat out of the afternoon and evening.'

'Clairvoyance?'

'He overheard Miss Tate in Sainsbury's coffee shop offering a lift to a friend. A woman much like herself, I gather. He'd still like you to tail Hutton, but suggests you stand down until the evening. Say nine o'clock.'

'Uhuh. Tied up now, is he?'

Phyllida understood the mixture of hurt and defiance in Steve's tone. 'He's still following Amy Tate around, that's why he asked me to contact you. He decided to make his one call to me, to find out if his description of Miss Tate's friend or the name Matty meant anything to me from the Little Theatre. They don't. Peter didn't see anything unlikely in Miss Tate's Sainsbury's trolley, but he just thought she might be going on to do some errand connected with tonight. He'll stand down himself if and when she goes home.'

'And will you?'

'Yes, but I'll leave my car where it is and walk to the Square. I don't want to lose my parking space. I'll come back to it at nine. All right?'

'Fine.' The cheery monosyllable was the

reward for Phyllida's tact, and made her decide to go on.

'Steve—'

'Yep?'

Phyllida dropped her voice. 'Melanie'll be especially appropriate tonight. Show your appreciation by spending the afternoon with her too.'

'Is that an order?'

'Of course not. I'm not in a position to give you orders. Call it a piece of interfering female advice. But think about it.'

'Okay, okay.'

'Thanks, Steve. Out.'

'What was that about?' Melanie enquired apprehensively. 'Change of plan?'

'Sort of. The boss has found out where the business is taking place, so we can stand down till the evening.' Steve surveyed the girl speculatively and ran a finger down her spine. 'So how about an afternoon nap at my place?' It might not be what Miss Moon had had in mind, but it would certainly suit Melanie.

At just short of eleven thirty that night there was a jostle of parking cars to both sides of the short slope leading from the main road west out of Seaminster to the sandy walkers' track into which the Parade a couple of miles back had degenerated. Each member of the Agency staff welcomed the sight of their subjects signalling their intention of joining it, then drove past. Each of them turned to the right up the first road inland, where Phyllida parked and the other two passed her with a salute.

When, following Peter's call, she had left the hire car in Horton Street, Miss Bowden had walked to the Golden Lion, picked up Phyllida's car, and driven it a mile beyond Red Rocks, where she had started to investigate possible parking places. She had been pleased to discover a series of short steep roads inland from the main road out of town, bounded at their foot by dunes that gave way to houses and then a few shops towards the top of each slope before it debouched on to the western end of Sea-minster's retail centre.

Phyllida parked outside the first group of small shops in the first road past the assembling cars, and watched Melanie's staring white face follow Peter's brake lights out of sight. When her watch reached eleven thirty-five she got out of her car and started silently down the slope on Miss Bowden's sensible rubber-soled shoes.

A few of the assembling cars had been forced to park on the main road, but all were now deserted, as were the cars on the lower slope down to the sandy track. Phyllida was able to observe these from several feet above, from the safety of the rough path through more dunes that paralleled the descent of the road where the cars were parked.

The dunes ended flush with the end of the road, on a stretch of bushes and stunted trees high enough to conceal a slightly crouched Phyllida from the sight of anyone looking up from the shore. But the shore was deserted, and the worn set of stone steps twisting down to it, and as Phyllida settled as well as she could into her uncomfortable hiding place she could only think the beach at that point must recess under the cliff, where there might be caves.

Phyllida was wondering how long she should wait before venturing on to the stone staircase when she heard a series of loud triumphal shouts and watched an eruption of white figures across the gleaming sands, still wet from the receding tide. Some of them were holding hands, others took hands as they ran. After a few moments of running and shouting, about ten of them formed a circle and started dancing round. Phyllida had to shake herself out of her disbelief and the drenching sense of bathos before she could reach for her tiny binoculars, and when she saw that the largest naked body in the circle belonged to Amy Tate she reached for her tiny camera and took a few shots before returning to the binoculars. Most of the figures were unfamiliar to her, but she recognised Clive Simpson and a couple of the women she had seen in the Little Theatre green-room without learning their names. And there was Henry Hutton, aloof but watchful, and Carol Swain and Paul Harper running towards Ben Carson—

Phyllida's binoculars fell from her hands as another pair of hands clamped her shoulders and a fierce whisper in her ear told her to keep quiet. In the next few seconds her gun as well as her camera were out of her deep pocket.

'You can pick up your spying glass, but don't try anything.'

'I won't.' Still numb with shock, Phyllida retrieved her binoculars.

'Now turn round.'

Phyllida obeyed, and found herself looking into the stern face of June Jones. It took her a few seconds to realise that Miss

Jones could not know they had met before and that despite appearances she had the advantage. A few feet behind them, a tall man in a raincoat was trying to make himself look small against a hillock of dune.

'I'm Detective Sergeant June Jones of Seaminster CID. And this is Detective Constable Chalmers.' Two cards flashed. 'Now, if you'll come with us.'

'I'm sure I don't have to.'

'I think it would be wise.'

Phyllida shrugged. 'Okay.' She wanted to go with them, of course, but not to seem eager.

The police car was parked only yards below her own. DC Chalmers got into the driving seat after seeing his DS and Phyllida into the back.

'Well, now,' Miss Jones said as the driver's door closed. 'What have you to say for yourself?'

'Must I say anything? Was I committing an offence?'

'I don't know. If you weren't, you won't mind telling me who you are, and if you have a licence for your gun. If you don't tell us here, we'll take you to the station and ask you again. That's hardly unreasonable.'

'No.' Phyllida had never felt more grateful

173

to anyone than she felt at that moment to Miss Bowden. 'All right. My name's Mary Bowden and I work for the Peter Piper Private Detective Agency. So I have a licence for my gun. The Agency has been retained by the father of one of those naked bodies to investigate the possibility of his son being into drugs as a user or a dealer. The investigation is of the Little Theatre Company, where the police made a recent arrest.'

Phyllida had hoped for some reaction to her mention of the theatre, and received it in a reflex jerk of the body beside her. But DS Jones said calmly that it was a good story.

'Which I'd hardly make up. Look, there's no point in my giving you the Agency number because you'll still want to look it up for yourself. I'll be happy to come with you to your station and wait there while you do. You might even find my boss will answer the telephone tonight; he sometimes sleeps over. Peter Piper.'

There had been another sharp movement. 'Very well. On our way, Jack.'

'You took photographs,' June Jones said sternly as they moved off.

'Yes. Did you?'

'We shall want to see them.'

'We shall be happy to give you copies.' It was probably as cheeky as she should get, even with her confidence of having the last word. DS Jones made no rejoinder, and the rest of the short journey passed in silence.

'Picked up spying on a nudist beach party,' was the next thing she said, to the duty sergeant in the station. 'Claims to be a private eye.'

The duty sergeant asked for her name and address, and Phyllida told him Miss Mary Bowden of the Peter Piper Agency and the Golden Lion Hotel, both in Dawlish Square.

'You're saying you live at the Golden Lion?' DS Jones and DC Chalmers had jumped to attention, too.

'That's right.' There was nowhere else Mary Bowden lived.

The duty sergeant asked her to be good enough to turn out her pockets, and Phyllida put her binoculars, her camera, a notebook, a pen, her car keys and a bundle of tissues on the counter. 'My car's parked just in front of where yours was. You didn't give me time to write anything in my notebook. Look, ring the Agency as I suggested, in case my boss is there.' Phyllida quoted the number. 'Check it in the directory. Even if there's no reply I don't believe you can hold me; you know I haven't committed a crime.'

DS Jones turned on her heel without comment, and the duty sergeant tentatively suggested Miss Bowden sit down for the time being with the DC for company. 'It's an unusual situation,' he admitted, with a helpless smile, and asked the DC to fetch Miss Bowden a cup of tea. Phyllida was draining it when June Jones reappeared and told her crossly that she'd spoken to a man who said he was Peter Piper of the Peter Piper Detective Agency and that his field assistant was called Mary Bowden.

'You can go home,' the DS said grudgingly. 'DC Chalmers will take you to your car. We'd like to see you in the morning,' she added, as Phyllida picked up her belongings. 'With Mr Piper.'

'Of course. There's just one thing.'

'Well?'

Peter might have already said it, but if he hadn't, it would still, Phyllida reckoned, be better said. Better that they told him direct, than that he got to hear about it. 'I'd be grateful if you could put a note on Chief Superintendent Kendrick's desk to the effect that Peter Piper and Mary Bowden have been summoned to the station.'

'And why should I do that?'

It was not the moment, but Phyllida found herself admiring the voice again, warmed now by anger.

'Because I promise you he'll want to know. Just a note. Without comment, please.' Phyllida paused, then asked what time she and Peter should come to the station the next morning and watched the DS fighting her curiosity.

'Ten thirty,' DS Jones said, losing the fight. Phyllida would have taken a bet that the DS had intended saying nine a.m., but ten thirty would ensure that the Chief Superintendent had time to read the note before she and Peter arrived.

DC Chalmers drove her to her car via the top road, and she drove back to the Golden Lion via the lower and saw that all the cars had gone from the slope down to the sea. But the wind had strengthened and the air temperature had fallen by several degrees.

# Ten

Phyllida went straight to the office on her release, and straightaway asked Peter a question. She had begun to wonder, as the pleasure of mentioning the Chief Super-intendent to DS Jones ebbed, if she had been out of line, and it was a relief to learn that Peter, too, had suggested that a note be left for Kendrick.

'That makes me even more in awe of Sergeant Jones's self-control. She didn't give me the least idea that she'd already been asked.'

'Is that all it is, d'you think?' Peter asked wistfully. 'Naturism?'

'I suppose we ought to hope so. It certainly fits with Miss Tate and her friend Matty. Probably the most exciting thing either of them has ever done in their entire lives. Carson and Carol Swain... Well, I've known bright young things in my time for whom to be naked in company was im-portant. And I should say young Paul is pretty impressionable.'

'But dancing on a beach with nothing on isn't enough, surely, to account for a change of personality?'

'I wouldn't think so, but I suppose it could be a symbol of it. DS Jones, by the way, gave me no indication of whether the nudist gathering was a surprise to her, or a disappointment, or neither. I wonder if the Chief Superintendent will do anything beyond tearing his hair?'

'We'll soon know.' Peter poured the drinks.

'I'll stay at the hotel again tonight. I'll need Miss Bowden in the morning, and I still feel I'm in the middle of something, although I don't know what it is.'

Peter rang across the Square just before ten the next morning, when Miss Bowden was nearly ready.

'They don't want us. It was a minion who rang, but it has to be Kendrick's decision.'

'It would have choked DS Jones to make the call. Ah, well.'

'It's not as disappointing as it sounds,' Peter coaxed. 'Kendrick may not feel he needs to see us, but he's deflected DS Jones's wrath and he hasn't warned us off the theatre. Those two negatives make a positive.'

'I suppose so.'

'We can be sure of one thing.' Phyllida heard amusement in Peter's voice. 'The Chief Superintendent will be wondering if the Little Theatre Company has one particular new recruit.'

'He'd only have to find out that a mature American lady has recently joined, and he'd know.'

'But DS Jones won't be telling him, will she, because she doesn't know it's relevant. Cheer up.'

'I'm all right. It's just that I feel all dressed up with nowhere to go.'

Since his wife Miriam and his daughter Jenny had come back to him, Detective Chief Superintendent Kendrick's all-consuming joy and relief had slightly lengthened the fuse of his natural impatience. So that when one of his detective inspectors decided that in view of the Chiefs particular interest in the Little Theatre drugs case – stemming from his particular dislike of drug dealing – DS Jones's negative findings should be conveyed to him immediately, Kendrick's frustration and disappointment proved to be soluble overnight in his wife's embrace. But when he turned round from hanging his jacket on the old-fashioned coat tree behind his office door the following morning, and read the note awaiting him on his desk, he felt the old heat flaring behind his eyes. He stood for a moment with clenched fists and bent head before he could force himself to remember the help that had come each time in the past out of Miss Bowden's disconcerting intervention.

When he had managed to absorb the fact that their business paths had crossed yet again, he called for DS Jones.

'This note,' he said without preliminary, tapping it. 'You say you picked her up watching those thespian nudists last night?' He had to fight a grotesque desire to ask her what Miss Bowden had looked like.

'Yes, sir. Complete with gun. Her story was—'

'I know her story, Sergeant Jones. And I can vouch for it.' Kendrick studied his junior officer's blank face, and congratulated her in his mind for her self-control while unfairly finding it chilly. 'Perhaps you'll be good enough to arrange for the Peter Piper Agency to receive an immediate telephone call to the effect that neither Miss Bowden nor Mr Piper will be required to attend the station this morning.'

'Very good, sir.'

'That's all, thank you, Sergeant.'

But that was not all, of course, in the Chief Superintendent's head. With his memories of his previous encounters with Miss Bowden and her manifestations still uncomfortably vivid, Kendrick found himself, to his annoyance, intensely curious as to the appearance of the woman he alone knew would have infiltrated the Little Theatre Company, and whether she and the woman DS Jones had apprehended were the same person. Despite the assurances of Peter Piper and no real evidence to the contrary, Kendrick was still not quite able to accept that the various females he had encountered under the guise of Piper's field operative were one and the same. Sometimes he thought he had managed it, only for a new manifestation, wildly different in age as well as height and girth and voice, to throw him back into doubt.

One thing, at least, he believed to be consistent about Miss Bowden: she and her boss had convinced him by their conduct in the past that if in the course of their investigations they discovered something he would wish to know, they would tell him. Which meant that if in obedience to his word they failed to present themselves, then they had also failed to discover any further drug connections within the Little Theatre Company. This would be satisfactory for his ego, if not for his crusading desire to eliminate drug dealing from Seaminster, but it would also mean (on a trivial level, he was all too well aware) that unless he could get a description from someone – last night's duty sergeant? – of Miss Bowden's appearance, he would never know if it was an appearance he would have recognised, or yet another new one.

Chief Superintendent Kendrick spent his working day with question marks about Miss Bowden buzzing about his head like a tiresome swarm of flies. The duty sergeant who had seen her was not back at the desk until late afternoon, and when it came to the point Kendrick found himself sane enough not to approach him, or to question DS Jones or the DI who had put him in the picture. His day, not offering much in the way of distraction, seemed very long, and it was a relief to get home and confess what he was uncomfortably aware were his idiotic preoccupations to Miriam.

But it was she who notched them up by gently suggesting, after listening to him for some time in silence, that the means of satisfying his curiosity were in his own hands.

'And not just your curiosity, darling. If you speak to Piper and Miss Bowden you might discover they know something they're not aware of knowing, which could be a help to you. Maurice–' She took his hands in hers. 'Isn't your pride standing in the way of both these possibilities? Think about it.'

No one apart from his senior officers long ago had ever spoken to him so frankly, and although he and Miriam had been back together now for several months, Kendrick still felt the fearless straightness of her like a draught of water to a man who has thirsted a long time in the desert.

'Is it? D'you think it is?' But he already knew she was right, had half known it before she had spoken.

Miriam nodded, smiling.

'Very well. I'll call them both in first thing tomorrow. Now, perhaps I've earned a rest from them until then.'

In the event, it was late morning before the Chief Superintendent telephoned the Peter Piper Agency, because he had been in the office barely half an hour when Detective

Sergeant Jack Dee came to tell him that a dead body had been reported in the green-room of the Little Theatre Company, and that foul play was suspected.

'The caretaker discovered it early this morning, sir, after finding that the outer door had been unlocked all night. We just thought – while it's *in situ* – with your particular interest in the drug situation ... I've asked them not to move anything until you tell them to go ahead.'

'That was imaginative thinking, Jack, I appreciate it.' Kendrick wondered ruefully if part of his excitement was being certain for once that he was ahead of Miss Bowden. 'Yes, I'd like to pay a visit to the theatre. You can take me. Can you fill me in on the way?'

'I'm sorry, sir. I've told you all I know.'

And all Kendrick discovered when he first arrived at the theatre were the physical details and the name on the credit cards. The SOCO, forensics, the photographer and the doctor were in attendance, but a member of the Company who could formally identify the corpse was still awaited.

'We had a look at a few papers in the so-called office, sir, and found the phone number of the secretary. We've sent a car for her.'

'Good. Now, what have you found, Willy? Drugs?'

The doctor, who was overweight and nearing his retirement, puffed his way up from his knees. 'Not about his person, Maurice. And probably not inside him, from the look of his eyes, although I can't be sure what he's ingested, of course, until I do the post-mortem.'

'Did that kill him?' The man was on his back with a long slim handle protruding from his chest, but the Chief Super-intendent had learned long ago that appearances in this sort of situation could be deceptive.

'It did. Whether by luck or intention, the one thrust entered the heart. Death would have been instantaneous.' Dr Willis peered down at the weapon. 'Could be a stage prop. We found this.' He held up a plastic bag containing a small dark object Kendrick was unable to recognise. 'Blade shield. Damn dangerous, all the same, to have something like that lying about. I suppose they like to flash it around on the stage. This isn't the first time–'

The doctor broke off at the sound of a commotion in the doorway, and the two men turned to see a young woman break through the attempt to restrain her and start running towards the body. Half-way there, she screamed.

'Whoa, lass!'

As he, too, put out a deterrent hand, Kendrick irrelevantly recalled from the doctor's choice of sobriquet that he was a Yorkshireman. 'Steady on!' he said gently, but using sufficient strength to hold her clear of the body.

'It's all right, sir.' One of the forensic team followed her across. 'We've finished.'

'Then leave us for a few moments, will you?' Kendrick asked. 'Then you can take him away.'

'Very good, sir.' The little group of men and women disappeared silently through the door back into the foyer, and Kendrick and the doctor half carried the young woman away from the dead man. He had fallen against one of the small tables regularly spaced round the sides of the room, displacing a couple of chairs, and they led her to a table a little way off, helping her into a chair between the two they then took themselves and each maintaining his hold on an arm in a gesture that was half reassurance and half restraint.

'Who is it, lass?' the doctor coaxed.

The girl looked from him to Kendrick and back again, wild-eyed. 'It's Ben. My fiancé. My Ben. Tell me I'm dreaming!'

'Dear God... Oh, lass.' The doctor moved his hand professionally to the girl's wrist as Kendrick began to speak.

'Tell me your name,' he said softly.

'I'm Carol Swain. For God's sake–'

'When did you last see your fiancé, Miss Swain?'

'Last night. He was here, I was here, it was Amy's birthday. Angela Simpson had made a cake. It wasn't a party, just the committee and one or two... Please, let me–'

'I'm sorry, Miss Swain, but there's nothing you can do for him.' Kendrick and the doctor had both, on a reflex, tightened their grip. 'Did you and Mr Carson leave the theatre together?'

'What?' She turned to Kendrick with a puzzled air, as if she was only just aware of him.

'Did you and your fiancé leave the theatre together?'

'No. He knew I was driving over to spend the night with my mother, which I do on my own because she's the classic possessive mother and doesn't like sharing me.' The girl gave a great dry sob that shook her body. 'She won't have to worry about that now, will she?'

'Please go on,' Kendrick said, after a few seconds' silence in which the girl stared unseeingly into space. 'We'll take you home in a moment,' he added, in response to a shake of the doctor's head. 'Or wherever you want to go. Just tell me: when you left, was Mr Carson still here?'

'Everyone was. I left early because of driving to my mother's. I remember looking at Ben as I went out, and Ben looking at me... Oh, God.' The girl leapt to her feet, so suddenly and violently the men's hands fell away. 'I'm dreaming. I have to be!'

'So far as you know,' Kendrick said, he and the doctor rising too and each retrieving an arm, 'did Ben have any enemies?'

'Ben? Enemies? Don't be ridiculous! Ben was the kindest, sweetest... Someone must have been playing about with that wretched knife and thought the shield was on and it wasn't.'

It seemed to Kendrick that her blonde beauty was dropping away from her by the second, her face thinning as it paled, her bright blue eyes growing steadily out of proportion to their tensing surround. He'd seen it before with comely mourners of

189

violent death, both male and female, and he hated it. 'Perhaps someone was. Could it have been you, Carol? If it was an accident it would be much better–'

Carol Swain rounded on Kendrick, the huge eyes blazing. 'I told you, everyone was still here when I left! And if it *had* been me, d'you think I'd have gone off and left him? My darling Ben?'

'Perhaps, if you were sure he was dead. And if your suggestion about an accident is right, that would have to be what happened. No one reported the death.'

'I can't tell you what happened. I can only tell you that when I left Ben was fine.'

'Was the knife lying around?'

'In a way.' The girl's eyes slid away from Kendrick's. 'It was just... Someone suggested using it to cut Amy's birthday cake. Oh, no...' The slight body sagged, and the doctor put his arms under it, shaking his head again at Kendrick

'Do you remember who that person was?' the Chief Superintendent asked.

'Yes,' she whispered. 'It was Ben. Ben got the knife out and took the sheath off and handed the knife to Amy, and when she'd cut the cake it was Ben who took it from her and put it down on the bar top. Without its sheath, because it was sticky and needed washing before it could be sheathed and put away. The others will tell you; we were all watching.'

'Were you in the habit of playing with the knife?'

'No! We treated it with respect, we all knew how sharp it was. We weren't supposed to take the sheath off except when we were using it on stage. It was just ... Ben is – was – always very responsible, but it was a party, there was champagne, and I suppose he just felt–' Carol Swain's voice choked into silence.

'Thank you, Miss Swain. I'll need to talk to you again, of course, but you need to rest now.' Dr Willis nodded sternly. 'The doctor will see you out to one of our cars. Constable!' Kendrick called across to the door, and the tall young policeman standing there came smartly across to him. 'Miss Swain's to be taken home, or wherever she wants to go, with a WPC. And I want to see everyone else who was at last night's do here in this theatre no later than this afternoon. Miss Swain,' he said more gently, 'can you tell us the name of someone else who knows who was here last night?'

'What?' Again Carol Swain had gone away

from them, and Kendrick had to repeat himself before she was able to focus her wandering eyes on him.

'Oh, Amy. Amy Tate. Or Henry Hutton. They're joint Chairs. Or Clive Simpson, our Treasurer. You'll find their phone numbers in the office. Please–'

'Thank you, Miss Swain. You're leaving now. Just tell the driver where you want to go.' Kendrick turned to the waiting constable. 'You can tell the team they can come back in to finish up, and then you can find one of those three telephone numbers.'

During his moment of solitary waiting the Chief Superintendent went over to the body and stood looking down at it. The deep-set dark eyes were open, and he fancied there was a look of surprise in the darkly handsome face. But it would always be a surprise, surely, to realise one was about to be murdered.

Someone coughed behind him, and he turned round.

'Is there anything we can tell you, Chief?' the head pathologist asked. She was a tough and competent woman, still young, for whom Kendrick had a lot of respect.

He shook his head. 'I can tell *you*, though, Kate,' he said, 'not to be puzzled if you find a sweet edible substance on the knife. It was used last night to cut a cake and may not have been washed, or washed properly.'

A use which everyone present had witnessed, Kendrick thought wearily as he left the building. And seen the knife being put carelessly down on the bar counter afterwards by the murdered man. Pending the post-mortem findings, everyone would have to be asked if he or she had washed it, resheathed it, and put it away. Because that could have happened; the fact that it had been out and about and in use could have been enough to put something into someone's mind, so that he or she brought the knife out again. Or, of course, it could have been left lying on the bar top and the murderer had simply put out his or her hand. If there was evidence of cake in the wound–

*It wasn't a party. Just the committee and one or two...*

Kendrick brightened at the memory of Carol Swain's words, and the pleasure of being out in the sunshine drawing deep breaths and looking over a blue-green sea, but his spirits sank again as it occurred to him that Miss Bowden could have been among those one or two non-members of the Little Theatre committee who had watched the co-Chair cut her birthday cake with a murder weapon. He had to struggle to bring them up again with the realisation of the enormous help she would be to him if she had been present.

It was the first question Kendrick asked her after he had told her and her boss to sit down, and had given himself the length of time it took to pour coffee to take in her current manifestation. The bewilderment that had hit him at the sight of yet another persona grew as he covertly studied a woman so unremarkable he would never be sure, when he saw her again, that they had already met. And it was soon joined by the familiar irritation as he realised he was no nearer being certain whether Miss Bowden was one woman, or any number of them.

'No, Chief Superintendent. I didn't even know about it.' Her voice was as much of a turn-off as her appearance. 'But my American lady – Mrs Sonia Sheridan – has been made very welcome by the Little Theatre Company. As well as being cast in Henry Hutton's new play, she's been invited to join the regular informal weekly get-togethers and has already been to one.'

Which was more, Kendrick told himself,

than his DS Jones had managed. But he knew why... To his further irritation, Kendrick found himself having to close his inner eye against the picture conjured up by the words 'American lady' spoken by this dreary woman with the flat vowels: unwillingly, he had been attracted by Miss Bowden's earlier American persona, and he found himself now vividly recalling her and her perfume.

'Your DS Jones has a very fine voice. She and Mrs Sheridan read a scene together at the auditions – Viola and the Countess Olivia from *Twelfth Night* – and got a burst of spontaneous applause. I realise now that when they were both apparently studying the art display in the green-room her ear was cocked as keenly as mine.' Phyllida hesitated. 'I'd rather DS Jones didn't know about Mrs Sheridan's connection with Miss Bowden, Chief Superintendent.'

'So would I,' Kendrick responded shortly, picturing that chilly face if he should tell DS Jones that the Peter Piper Detective Agency employed a chameleon. 'I take it that the informal get-together didn't yield anything you felt you should report to me?'

'It yielded me the knowledge that there was to be a secret meeting, but not what it was about. If it had turned out to be to do with drug taking or dealing, Mr Piper would of course have informed you. If your DS hadn't surprised me I wouldn't have troubled you with a story about nudists on a beach.'

'Until, I hope, you had discovered via the media that the beach party had been followed by the murder of one of its participants.'

Kendrick was watching Miss Bowden keenly, and was gratified to see shock break through the impersonal calm of her face and be certain at last of one thing about her: he had seen the reaction of a real woman.

If only for an instant: Miss Bowden's face was again without expression as she spoke, and her voice was still flat. 'What are you saying, Chief Superintendent?'

Peter Piper asked Kendrick if he was saying a murder had taken place on the beach.

'No. It took place in the green-room at the Little Theatre, last night or very early this morning. The victim was a young man called Ben Carson, who was stabbed with a stage knife which was usually sheathed but had been unsheathed to cut the cake at the birthday party I mentioned. You've met Mr Carson of course, Miss Bowden?'

'Yes. Each time Mrs Sheridan has been to the theatre. He's – he was – a member of the casting committee.'

'And a friend of Paul Harper, the boy whose father's retained me,' Peter took up. 'Harper senior was worried–'

'I've seen Miss Bowden's statement,' Kendrick interrupted. 'There are only two things I need to ask her now.'

Peter and Phyllida just managed not to turn and look at one another. 'Yes?' Peter supplied.

Reluctantly Kendrick turned back to the woman. 'I would like you to tell me if there is the slightest thing you have seen or heard at the Little Theatre which makes you continue to believe in the possibility of an ongoing situation there to do with drug dealing or taking. Or else to assure me categorically that with your nudist conspiracy revealed you are unaware of anything left unexplained.'

'I can give you that assurance, Chief Superintendent.' Phyllida hadn't had to think about it. 'With the proviso you've already mentioned: if your DS Jones hadn't discovered the beach party, I – we – would have told you about it when we heard about the murder of Ben Carson.' This time

Phyllida did look towards Peter, who was looking towards her and nodding.

The Chief Superintendent thanked them, and Peter asked him if they were to take it that both the things he needed to ask Miss Bowden had been covered.

'No.' This part would never get any easier, and Kendrick got to his feet and took a brief, reassuring look over the sea, framed in the big window behind his chair. 'No,' he repeated, turning round but remaining on his feet. 'I want to ask her if she is prepared to continue as a member of the Little Theatre Company until the killer of Ben Carson is found, and to report to me anything she feels may be relevant to the murder investigation. If she agrees, I will of course retain her according to our – our previous financial arrangements, and I will ensure that your Agency is made aware of the facts surrounding the murder as far as we are aware of them ourselves.' Kendrick took a deep breath. 'Do you agree, Miss Bowden?'

Peter nodded again as Phyllida glanced at him. 'I do, Chief Superintendent. I accept both your assignment and the condition attached to it.' Phyllida smiled to herself as she heard her acceptance in the words that came naturally to Mary Bowden, wondering how Mrs Sheridan would have expressed herself. The American woman would certainly have done her best to spare the Chief Superintendent from feeling like a suppliant, but such sensitivity – and that kind of skill – were not in Miss Bowden's nature.

On a frisson of dismay, Phyllida reminded herself that, of all her characters, only Miss Moon was real.

## Eleven

Kendrick's reflex reaction was a leap of the heart when at two thirty p.m. that afternoon he and his DS Ted Wetherhead found just six people awaiting them in the Little Theatre green-room. But he immediately chided himself for his naivety: this could be merely the more public-spirited contingent.

'Where are the others?' he enquired sternly of the uniformed constable in attendance.

'There are no others, sir.'

'We're all here, Chief Superintendent!' The constable's quiet response was all but drowned by the proclaimed statement of the largest of the women, advancing to meet Kendrick with a fat white hand extended. Reluctantly he shook it. 'Amy Tate. Chair – co-Chair–' the amendment followed a brittle cough from the tall thin man beside whom the woman had been standing '–of the Little Theatre Company.' A further cough had her half turning and extending her hand backwards. 'Mr Henry Hutton, my co-Chair.' Miss Tate's sensibly shod feet followed her hand back to the small standing group. 'Allow me also to introduce Mr Clive Simpson, our stage manager, his wife, Angela, and Mr Paul Harper. Oh, and–' obviously on an afterthought, Miss Tate undid her move back towards the Chief Superintendent 'Miss Matilda Thompson. You'd better sit down, Paul,' she concluded, concern entering her voice as it dropped in volume. She took the youngest member of the group, a tall handsome youth with a lot of fair hair and a face rosy and swollen from weeping, by the hand. 'Paul and Ben were close friends,' she told the policemen in a stage whisper, when she had helped the boy to a chair, sat him down, and was standing with her hand on his shoulder. 'This is a terrible tragedy, Chief Superintendent.'

'Indeed,' Kendrick responded drily. 'Now, I suggest we all sit down, my sergeant and myself included, while you fill me in on the party that ended with the death of Mr Carson.' He paused while Ted Wetherhead and PC Russell moved a second table against the one at which he was sitting, and rearranged chairs. 'I'll be talking to each of you separately, of course,' he continued when they were settled, 'but perhaps a few questions while we're all together will help me get a picture of the evening.' Kendrick looked round the silently waiting group, trying as he always did to interpret their tension. Because each of them, innocent or guilty, had to be tense.

Miss Tate had seated herself beside Paul Harper and was holding his hand. Kendrick noted that the boy's was immobile in her clasp, and that it was Miss Tate's fingers that were restlessly twitching, although her face appeared serene and brightly expectant. Miss Thompson, in contrast, looked frightened and unhappy and kept glancing towards the profile with which Miss Tate consistently presented her. Clive Simpson, classically red-haired with freckled pink skin, sat upright and alert, ignoring the small birdlike woman beside him whose pursed lips kept relaxing and who, Kendrick suspected, had to keep reminding herself that she was involved in a real-life tragedy and not an exciting fictional murder mystery. The most intriguing member of the group, for Kendrick, was the co-Chair of the Little Theatre Company, Henry Hutton, whose glittering dark eyes in the ascetically thin face, and occasional precisely fastidious movement, proclaimed the aesthete and the intellectual, whether genuine or self-styled Kendrick could not as yet venture to guess. But the one thing he already awaited with confidence was a jostling for position between the company's co-Chairs.

It came at once, after DS Wetherhead had told them that the caretaker had found the theatre building unlocked when he arrived that morning, and asked who had been the last to leave the evening before. Mr Hutton and Miss Tate, in duet and with irritated exchanges of looks, both declared that when the rest of the party left, more or less together, Ben Carson was still in the theatre. Kendrick was not surprised to find that Hutton's diction reminded him of Noel Coward, although the voice had more substance.

'Thank you.' Kendrick decided he'd have

to put up with it; coming down on one side or the other could impede the flow of the one he didn't select as spokesman.

'Ben said something about going to the loo,' Clive Simpson slipped in quickly. 'And that he'd lock up.'

'Thank you,' Kendrick repeated. 'So far as you all know, then, you left him alone in the theatre?'

'Weren't you waiting for him, Paul?' Henry Hutton enquired. 'Carol had left a little before us, if I remember rightly, but she had said something about visiting her mother. You came out with the rest of us, did you? I don't recall.'

The glitter in Henry Hutton's eyes had intensified, and Kendrick thought he had identified a mischief-maker.

'No, I wasn't waiting!' Paul Harper responded passionately, aroused from his listlessness, it occurred to Kendrick, by the sudden need for self-preservation. 'I didn't hear Carol say she had to go. I thought she was still in the building, too, and that she and Ben would leave together!'

'I remember Paul disappearing to the loo a little while before we broke up,' Amy Tate offered pacifically. 'He could have missed Carol's announcement.' The boy flung her a grateful glance, and Kendrick saw his hand tense round her mobile fingers, momentarily stilling them.

'Whether or not you left together,' he told them, 'let me remind you that the theatre doors were not locked last night. Any one of you could have come back before Carson left. What you were doing after you say you left the theatre together is what I shall be asking you in your individual interviews.'

'We *did* leave together!' To Kendrick's surprised admiration, Clive Simpson's meek-looking wife was suddenly bristling. 'And if the door was unlocked, *anyone* could have come in from the street and killed – killed – Oh, God.' Mrs Simpson was suddenly aware that the matter in hand was fact and not fiction. Her husband had to be a cold bastard, Kendrick decided: he hadn't so much as turned his head towards her.

'You're quite right, madam,' DS Wetherhead responded. 'But in a situation as serious as this the police have to have proof before we can be convinced that any – anyone–' Kendrick suspected that Ted had just saved himself from saying 'any suspect' – 'was where they say they were, and doing what they say they were doing. A moment's thought, and you'll–'

'That's all right, Sergeant,' Clive Simpson interrupted. 'I think we all understand.' At last he had put out a hand to his wife, but it was a warning gesture and Kendrick was glad to see that, despite her sudden anguish, the glance with which she responded was not submissive.

'Thank you, sir. Now,' Kendrick said. 'Did any of you notice anything about Mr Carson last night that seemed unusual? Did he appear to be his characteristic self?" He wouldn't ask them until they were alone with him and Ted whether they had seen anything they felt was uncharacteristic about any of their still living fellow-guests.

Paul Harper flashed an immediate and passionate 'No!' which was followed by more tempered, but equally unequivocal, negatives from everyone else.

'Miss Swain was taken home this morning after her ordeal,' Kendrick said. 'Before she went she told us that the knife which killed Mr Carson had been used to cut Miss Tate's birthday cake.' He paused to watch the communal wave of guilty regret pass across the faces in front of him. 'She also made a suggestion which could explain Mr Carson's death. She suggested that, after she had left, someone might have picked up the knife from where it had been put down following the cake cutting, and made a joking feint at Mr Carson, perhaps believing the knife had been resheathed. A feint too far, which penetrated his heart, the knife being very sharp.' Kendrick paused, to look again at their faces, all of which appeared to express some degree of disappointment. 'When it was clear that Mr Carson was beyond help, you could have decided to depart together, deliberately leaving the outer door unlocked so that it would appear possible for someone to have entered the theatre from the street and killed him. Would anyone care to comment?'

'I wish that *was* what happened!' Miss Tate trumpeted. 'It would have been a terrible tragedy, but it wouldn't have been murder!' There was a murmur of assent, and Kendrick decided she had just explained the general disappointment.

'That's right,' he tempted. 'If it did happen like that it wouldn't be murder, it would be manslaughter at the most. And we couldn't prevent you assuming collective guilt, refusing to name the person who made the thrust. Such altruism would ensure very lenient sentences.' Kendrick stopped, and regarded them.

'If they don't take your offer up,' Ted Wetherhead whispered, 'then that's not how it happened.'

'I know,' Kendrick murmured. 'And they're not going to, although they're all looking – or making themselves look – as if they wish they could. Ben Carson was murdered, Ted.'

For the individual interviews, Kendrick separated the tables and retained just three chairs at the one where he and Ted sat down, grateful for the relaxed and up-holstered ambience where their suspects were used to being at their ease. After telling the assembled group that he was not anticipating keeping any of them for long, he had asked them if they would be good enough to await their turn in the rehearsal room. A whispered word from the uni-formed constable about the layout of the company's space made him add that per-haps they would like to visit their respective cloakrooms before they were shut in, to avoid interruption of the individual inter-views.

Kendrick noted a few covert glances, but no one took him up on his invitation, and he told them they could come through to him

and the sergeant in the order they themselves chose – a concession which was, of
course, a further insurance on his part that
he would not appear to be favouring one co-
Chair at the expense of the other.

After a few moments the closed door to
the rehearsal room opened and the other fat
lady came tripping through and dithered
her way up to the policemen.

'Miss...?' DS Wetherhead enquired
politely, after eliciting an infinitesimal shake
of the head from his superior. 'I'm afraid I
don't–'

'Thompson. Matilda Thompson,' came
breathlessly tumbling out. 'I'd never met Mr
Carson before last night. I was here as a
friend of Amy's, not as a member of the
theatre company.'

'You could have been both,' Kendrick
joked. 'Now, there's no need to be nervous,
Miss Thompson.' As a friend of Miss Tate's
Miss Thompson might have attended the
nude bathing party, which could account, in
part at least, for her palpable panic. So far as
his DS Jones had been able to discover – on
a flash of irritation Kendrick wondered if
Miss Bowden had done better – five people
at Amy Tate's birthday party had been at the
beach party too, and four of them, perhaps

208

plus Miss Thompson, would now be afraid that the investigation of the murder of someone who had also been present could bring their eccentricity to light, maybe through a diary that named names. Could bring more to light than eccentricity. In view of the beach party's chronological proximity to the birthday party, he would soon be fulfilling the fears of four of them – but with the assurance that unless a connection was found between the recent drugs arrest and/or the murder of Ben Carson, the police were not in a position to take action against them. One of Kendrick's older uniformed sergeants had informed him of the ancient right of nude assembly on the stretch of beach involved, and was even at that moment seeking written confirmation of it in Seaminster's reference library.

Kendrick had been silent for too long, and DS Wetherhead was asking Miss Thompson if she had left the theatre with Miss Tate.

'Yes. Amy picked me up from home, and she took me straight back there. I asked her if she'd like to come in for a cup of cocoa, but she said it was late and just dropped me off.'

'Did anyone else go with you?' Kendrick asked.

'No.'

'Did you see how the other party guests left? Who was with whom? In cars or on foot?' There was no point in asking a self-proclaimed non-member of the Little Theatre Company if anyone had appeared to be behaving out of character. 'Just picture the scene for me if you will, Miss Thompson.'

'Try to relax,' DS Wetherhead contributed.

'Yes.' Miss Thompson screwed up her eyes as if her mental pictures were at the far end of the room. 'I'd met the – the dead man's fiancée, Carol Swain, before. She wasn't with us when we left; she'd gone earlier, as Amy said. I remember when we were in the car park seeing the young lad – Paul, isn't it? – sort of slouching towards a car with his hands in his pockets. On his own. And I remember Amy smiling when we saw Mr Hutton getting into an enormous old car; she said he was always saying there was no need to take a car on short journeys. He saw us watching him, I could tell, and sort of scuttled in and shut his door very quickly. I think that's all... Oh, Mr Simpson, the man with red hair, he and his wife went off on foot.'

'D'you know where they live?' DS Wetherhead enquired.

'I'm sorry, I've no idea.'

'Never mind!' Kendrick said bracingly. 'You've been most helpful, Miss Thompson.' He meant it: a factual comment on everyone who had been a guest at Miss Tate's party from someone whom he must, at that moment, presume to be objective was the best basis he could have hoped for to the other interviews. 'You can go now. When you've given your name and address to the uniformed officer.'

'May I wait for Amy?'

'By all means.'

'Thank you!' Miss Thompson was already on her feet and turning eagerly towards the rehearsal room and anticipated one-up-manship.

'When you've seen the constable, will you please wait in the foyer.'

'Oh. Yes.' Unable to hide her disappointment, Miss Thompson walked slowly across the green-room. As she opened the rehearsal room door the PC accosted her with a notebook and allowed the waiting sentinel figure of Clive Simpson to walk stiffly across to Kendrick and Wetherhead before writing down what Miss Thompson told him and indicating she should make her way out to the foyer along the opposite side of the green-room from where the interviews were taking place.

'Sit down, Mr Simpson,' DS Wetherhead invited, while Kendrick wondered on a flash of charity if the man might be coping as best he could with a back injury.

'Now,' he began. 'Did you and your wife come to the theatre by car last night, Mr Simpson?'

'No, Inspector.'

'Chief Superintendent,' DS Wetherhead murmured.

The sandy eyebrows rose. 'So this is a serious matter. Chief Superintendent.'

'Murder is always a serious matter,' Kendrick responded severely. 'And particularly so in a community inside which another serious crime has recently been committed.' Kendrick was aware of his DS's surprised reaction, but Simpson had to be chastised for implying that murder *per se* was not automatically heinous. 'So you and your wife did *not* come to the theatre by car last night?'

'That is correct, Chief Superintendent. We live close by – just round the corner in fact – and I only ever come by car when the weather is really bad, or I have something

212

bulky to bring with me.'

'I see. Thank you. What did you do when you got home?'

'We went to bed!'

Kendrick ignored the implied reproof. 'And you left with the others, minus Miss Swain, who had already left, and Mr Carson, who remained in the theatre?'

'Miss Swain certainly wasn't to be seen when we left, although I don't recall her leaving earlier, or talking about visiting her mother. But you'll appreciate, Chief Superintendent, that even though we were a small group we did break up during the evening and have separate conversations at the same time. I do remember Mr Carson telling us to go on and that he would lock up.'

'Thank you.' Kendrick's native pessimism told him that the witnesses were proving to be too good, and that the downside must soon redress the balance. 'You saw the others depart?'

'I saw them, so far as I can remember, leaving the theatre as my wife and I left. I'm afraid I didn't see them walk to their cars or drive away, because Angela and I almost immediately turned off from the Parade.'

'You saw the knife on the bar counter after the cake had been cut?'

Clive Simpson appeared to consider. 'I saw Ben put it down there after taking it from Amy when she'd cut the cake. I don't remember noticing it again.'

'So you didn't notice anyone wash it?' DS Wetherhead asked. 'Or wash it yourself?'

'No, Sergeant. I didn't.' Kendrick saw a muscle constrict in Simpson's cheek, but his voice was still stiffly polite.

'Did you notice anything in the behaviour of anyone which struck you at the time as unusual? Out of character?' DS Wetherhead asked.

Clive Simpson considered before speaking, but Kendrick had put the man down as a stickler and felt there need be no significance in the delay. 'No,' Simpson said at last. 'Everyone seemed just as usual.'

*As eccentric as usual? As bloody bonkers?* Kendrick enjoyed a few seconds of wondering what word or phrase had been in the stage manager's mind: the man had offered no clue.

'Thank you, Mr Simpson,' he said. 'When you've given your name and address to the uniformed constable you're free to leave. Although I expect you'll want to wait for your wife. In the foyer, please.'

'She'll be coming next,' Simpson told

them confidently, and when he opened the rehearsal room door she was waiting the other side of it beside PC Russell. Simpson put his hands on her upper arms and said something, but she twitched free and darted into the green-room and across to the detectives. Simpson remained in the doorway watching her until she had sat down and the PC had indicated the preferred route to the foyer.

Kendrick's observation of Angela Simpson's reactions during his talk to the assembled group had prepared him for a stronger show of character than her demeanour had at first suggested, and it came. Because Clive hadn't heard Carol say she was leaving early to go to her mother's didn't mean she hadn't said it. And anyway, *she* had heard Carol say just that, and seen her leave ten minutes or so before the rest of them.

'Thank you, Mrs Simpson, that's most helpful. Now, did you see Mr Carson put the knife down on the bar counter after Miss Tate had used it to cut her cake?'

'I remember her handing it back to him – he'd been the one to get it out of the props cupboard, because it was his idea to use it – but I don't remember actually seeing him

215

put it down. I suppose someone or something must have distracted me.' Mrs Simpson had been talking conversationally, and Kendrick saw the same change come over her face that he had seen when he had been addressing the group. 'My God,' she said. 'It's *awful*. We all wished it could be the way you suggested, Mr Kendrick. An accident. But it wasn't.'

'No. What did you do when you got home?'

'We went to bed.' Kendrick saw the surprise in her face turn to wariness and then to indignation.

'Just a routine question, Mrs Simpson,' he added swiftly, before the indignation could find expression. 'Thank you.'

Kendrick sat back, leaving Ted to make the usual concluding remarks while he tried to imagine what it must be like to be an innocent member of a group that has been devastated by murder. He'd been on the outside looking in for so many years, it always surprised – and annoyed – him that he never got anywhere near envisaging how it must feel to be on the inside.

The next arrival was the boy. He came across the room in the way Miss Thompson had described his approach to his car the night before – slouching with his hands in his pockets. When he reached the policemen he slumped down in the chair the DS indicated and looked from one to the other of them with an expression of pleading despair.

'I'm so very sorry,' Kendrick said, as gently as he could. 'I know Mr Carson was a close friend of yours.'

'Yes. He was.'

Paul Harper gave a deep, dry sob, and Kendrick was aware of Ted moving uneasily in his chair. His DS hated anyone to cry, particularly a man, but the danger moment passed as the boy took refuge in anger.

'It's wicked!' he flashed. 'It has to be some depraved creature who came in off the street! No one who knew Ben would have killed him! Not *Ben*.'

'Nor anyone else, I hope,' Kendrick added.

'Of course not!' Paul Harper responded impatiently. 'We're a group of civilised people.'

'None of whom appeared to you to be behaving in a way different from normal?' DS Wetherhead enquired.

'Of course not!' Harper repeated, this time with scorn. 'It'd been a super evening. Ben was happy, he'd made a good sale earlier on, and the day before he'd discovered a new painter. Oh, God...'

'Let it come,' Kendrick invited, on an apologetic glance at his discreetly squirming DS.

'I'm all right.' Kendrick had correctly gauged that the invitation might serve to strengthen the boy's resistance to breakdown. Paul Harper blew his nose and made a token gesture of sitting up straighter in his chair.

'Good man,' DS Wetherhead approved with relief. 'Now, did you see Mr Carson put the knife down on the bar counter after Miss Tate had cut her cake with it?'

'I think so. I know I saw it lying there, because I remember it crossed my mind that it would be sticky and ought to be washed before the sheath was put back on.'

'But you didn't see anybody do that, or wash it yourself?' Kendrick asked.

'No. I suppose I sort of thought Ben would do it ... Oh, God, I can't–'

'We've almost finished, Mr Harper. For the time being. Perhaps you can just tell us if you saw Miss Swain leave the party before the rest of you?'

'No! I've told you already! I never heard

her say she was going to her mother's, and I thought she was still in the building. That's why I didn't wait for Ben. If only I had.'

'I'm very sorry. You're certain that you and the other guests – apart from Mr Carson – left the building at the same time?'

'Yes.'

'Thank you.' DS Wetherhead took up. 'And did you see them disperse?'

'I saw Clive and his wife walking off along the Parade. They only live round the corner. And I must have seen Amy and her friend, and Henry, in the car park, because I remember being amused by the two fat ladies squeezing into a little car while Henry who's thin as a lath was climbing into a huge one. I actually drove off first, though.'

'And went home?'

'Yes.'

'And stayed there?'

'Yes! And went to bed!'

'Which your parents can vouch for?' It had just occurred to Kendrick that Paul Harper was the only one of Amy Tate's birthday party guests whose return home and retirement to bed might be verifiable by witnesses, and that if he could obtain that verification he would be able to eliminate one of his suspects.

But there was a flash of alarm across the boy's face. 'My parents are away. They're back this evening. But I went to bed! Anyway, it's obscene to think I could have killed Ben! It's disgusting!'

As with Mrs Simpson, alarm had been subsumed in indignation. But Paul Harper had more reason to be alarmed.

'It was just a routine query, Paul,' Kendrick responded soothingly. 'Now, here's another one. In your opinion, could there be a connection between your friend Ben's death and his nude presence on the beach a couple of nights ago, when you too were present?'

Paul Harper gave a choked cry, and his eyes stared wildly into Kendrick's from above the fist he had pushed against his mouth. DS Wetherhead advised him to take his time, and a few seconds went by before he spat out the word, 'Who?'

'None of your fellow nudists,' Kendrick assured him. 'Just police vigilance following the Little Theatre's recent woes. And nothing for any of you to worry about – the police are aware of the right of nude assembly on that stretch of beach, and we're not going to tell the media. It's just that your midnight party and your friend's death took place very close together. D'you think there's any connection?'

Paul Harper shook his head and lowered his hand. His mouth made Kendrick think of a child's mouth, swollen and trembling in the aftermath of a crying bout. 'No. It was a wonderful night. Happy. Like Amy's party. Oh, God.'

'You obviously haven't had time, though, to think about it properly in relation to Ben's death. If anything occurs to you, please get in touch with me.' DS Wetherhead had to push the Chief Superintendent's card into one of the hands now lying inert on the table edge. 'We shall probably want to speak to you again, anyway, but you can go now. After you've given your name and address to PC Russell.'

'OK.' Kendrick watched despair settle back over the boy's face as he got to his feet. Head bowed, he made his way slowly over to the rehearsal room, and as slowly across the green-room to the foyer after an exchange with the PC at the door and not a glance inside.

'He's very cut up,' DS Wetherhead commented as the door to the foyer swung to behind him. 'Could be shock as much as sorrow, of course. And the shock of his bare bottom secret being out must have been pretty strong.'

'Yes,' Kendrick agreed, managing, he hoped, to hide his satisfaction. 'Now, let's have a quick bet on which of the two principals manages to reserve the top of the bill spot.'

'I say Miss Tate.'

'I'm glad you say that, because I think Henry Hutton. I'm convinced he's without gallantry.'

Kendrick was right: as he finished speaking, Amy Tate emerged from the rehearsal room.

Whether being worsted by her co-Chair had subdued her, Miss Tate's manner was noticeably less ebullient than hitherto. But recalling her kindness towards the boy, Kendrick thought this might be accounted for by simple sorrow.

She gave them nothing not already given by the other people they had seen, but by this stage of the interviews Kendrick was confident of having secured all the information available and was seeking reactions rather than facts.

The question about the behaviour of fellow guests was therefore by now the most potentially interesting, but Miss Tate told them that no one had appeared to be acting in any way out of character. Asked what she had done when she got home, she said with the now familiar show of indignation that she had gone straight to bed.

'And no, Chief Superintendent, there is no one to support my statement. As there will be no one to support any of the other statements. Even young Paul's, as you have no doubt discovered, seeing that his parents are away.'

Her reaction to Kendrick's final question about a possible connection between the beach party and Ben Carson's death, which he coupled with the same assurance he had given Paul Harper, evoked an astonished denial which within seconds was replaced by what Kendrick could only describe to himself as a sort of defiant pride, succeeded in turn by a bridling indignation.

'So we have a traitor in our midst! Someone pretending to be one of us has betrayed our innocence! Chief Superintendent, the whole basis of our movement is a return to the Golden Age, to a time when–'

He was thankful to be in a position to cut her short. As he claimed police responsibility for his knowledge, and told her why it had been acquired, her face cleared to its usual bright serenity and she bowed her head as if in acknowledgement of an act of justice.

'I realise you haven't had enough time as yet to think about either party in relation to Mr Carson's death,' he went on. 'But if anything occurs to you that you think I should know...'

Her hand came out to accept his card.

Henry Hutton made much the same comment about there being no one to support his statement that he had gone home to bed, but without the indignation. 'You're probably going to have to take everyone's own word for it, Inspector–' DS Wetherhead's whispered correction had not been heeded – 'because apart from the Simpsons none of us, so far as I know, has a regular sleeping companion. And if any of us last night had an irregular one –' the glitter in the dark eyes again intensified – 'he or she might prefer not to make use of the fact.'

'Point taken, Mr Hutton. Did it seem to you that anyone at the party last night behaved out of character? Appeared to be unduly worried?'

Kendrick had seen enough of Henry Hutton to be prepared to take an affirmative with a pinch of salt, but after a few seconds' thought, and with a flash of regret across his face, Hutton shook his head.

'No, Inspector. I saw nothing beyond the usual eccentricities.'

'Did you see Mr Carson put the knife down on the bar counter after the cake cutting?'

'I did. I remember wishing he had washed it first.'

'Did anybody wash it? Did you wash it?'

'Certainly not. I had no wish to handle it. I detest knives almost as much as I detest firearms. So far as I know, no one touched it again.'

'Thank you. Now, Mr Hutton. One final question. Could there, in your opinion, be a connection between Mr Carson's death and his nude presence on the beach a couple of nights ago, when you too were present?'

The last reaction Kendrick had expected was amusement, but after a few seconds of blankness that was what Henry Hutton's impassive face faintly showed.

'So you're still looking for drug barons, Inspector! I trust you have also detected that we have the right of assembly on that particular stretch of beach?'

'We have, sir,' DS Wetherhead responded.

'I've scarcely had time to consider your question,' Hutton said to Kendrick. 'But I shall. I assure you I shall.'

'Thank you, sir.' It was a relief that Hutton had got there without help and had made no fuss, but as Kendrick put his card into the paper-dry hand he was amused to find himself with the feeling of having been cheated out of an ace.

When he had gone and they were packing up, the feeling of dissatisfaction lingered as a sense of unfinished business. Kendrick's amusement turned to chagrin when he interpreted it as regret that Peter Piper's sophisticated American had not been among the interviewees.

## Twelve

The first rehearsal of Henry Hutton's *Interrelations* was scheduled for the Monday evening following the Friday on which Ben Carson had been found dead, and in consultation with Peter, Phyllida decided to play ignorant – Sonia Sheridan, world citizen, could be forgiven for not reading the local paper of the place where she was temporarily perched, or seeing or listening to its local news. So, if a member of the Little Theatre Company telephoned her to announce the tragedy, she would be shocked and sorry. If she heard nothing she would present herself as arranged, and be shocked and sorry in person.

In the event, Tracy called her from the Golden Lion Reception late on Sunday afternoon to say that a Miss Tate had just rung to speak to Mrs Sheridan. Phyllida was spending the day restlessly at home, her mobile close at hand as she worked in house and garden.

'I told her you were due back any time,' Tracy said. 'So I should say you need only give it a few minutes, Miss Moon, before you ring back.'

'Thank you, Tracy.' Phyllida hesitated, then reminded herself that the integrity and intelligence of Tracy and her fellow receptionists had been well and truly proven over the past months. 'Tell me, has the murder at the Little Theatre made big local news?'

'I should say so! And people are linking it with the drug arrest. Inevitable, I suppose, with there being so little crime in Seaminster, and then two big ones in the same

227

place at almost the same time. But bad luck for the Company.'

'Yes.'

Miss Tate would take it with a canter, though. When she rang her back, Phyllida was unsurprised by the continuing buoyancy of her voice, although she was aware of the strain behind it. If ever there was an actress, professional or amateur, who deserved the name of trouper, it was Amy Tate.

'Mrs Sheridan. Perhaps you know why I'm ringing you?'

'I'm sorry... Oh, dear, have I missed the first rehearsal? I'd put Monday down.'

'It is Monday, Sonia. It's still Monday. Tomorrow. But I can see that you don't know why I've called you. I'm afraid there's some very bad, sad news. Ben Carson was found dead in the green-room on Friday morning. Stabbed. I'm afraid it's murder. I thought you might have–'

'I've been away most of the weekend, so I haven't... *How dreadful.* I'm afraid I'm not quite taking it in.'

'None of us are. It's a nightmare. And a mystery, an absolute mystery. Ben was a gentle soul and everyone loved him.'

'How awful for you all. I'm most dreadfully sorry, Amy. But you're not cancelling or postponing the production?'

'No! We're going ahead with it. We'll be destroyed by this latest blow if we don't. And Ben would have wanted us to.' And Henry Hutton also wanted them to, Phyllida inserted between Amy's respectful lines. His play cast, the bloodless author would be impatient of delay. 'And on a practical level, Ben wasn't going to be in it. Oh, dear, I didn't mean—' Miss Tate, perhaps quoting her co-Chair, had heard herself sound too practical.

'Of course you didn't.' Not for the first time, Phyllida was grateful for the soothing qualities of the husky American voice. 'And of course he would want you to go ahead. Oh, my goodness. Poor Carol!'

'Yes. She's very shocked. And poor young Paul, he really looked up to Ben.'

'Let's hope that in due course they can comfort one another.'

Amy Tate's, 'Yes,' sounded so doubtful Phyllida made a mental note to repeat her pious hope when she was in the theatre. 'So, I'll come as arranged then, shall I?'

'Please. That's from Henry, too. He particularly asked me to urge you not to be – well, deterred – by what's happened.'

229

Or Miss Jones. Seeing the Chief Superintendent's stern face before her mind's eye, Phyllida suspected that she, too, would be undeterred.

'Of course I'll come. And if I can be of any help to any of you in any way—'

'That's very kind of you, Sonia. You'll be a help just by joining us, bringing in some sanity. Reminding us that the world hasn't gone mad.'

'The police—'

'All the police appear to have done is to check with Carol's mother that the poor girl really did spend the night with her. But they could hardly ask my next door neighbour if she happened to be looking out of her window at half-past eleven on Friday night when I got home.'

'No... Oh, dear. It really is dreadful. But I mustn't keep you any longer, now. I'll see you tomorrow.' When it would be easier, face to face and with a number of informants, to appear to be discovering bit by bit what she had learned from Chief Superintendent Kendrick in a few moments about the eve of Ben's death.

Mrs Sheridan arrived at the Little Theatre promptly the next evening, to discover that DS Jones was already there. Phyllida was amused by her keenly suspicious gaze, particularly when it was followed by a dismissive shake of the head as Miss Jones transferred her attention to the people who were following Mrs Sheridan into the rehearsal room. Amy Tate, Henry Hutton and Clive Simpson were seated side by side on the small platform, a combined defiant statement that business was as usual, and for a bizarre moment Phyllida found herself looking for Ben and Carol to join them, the scene was so near what it had been on her last visit.

Except for the dismal atmosphere, which had its origins, it seemed to Phyllida, in the motionless drooping sphere of Miss Tate, whose huge bonhomie, despite her brave attempt to appear her usual self, was now so obviously eclipsed by a huge melancholy. Henry Hutton was clearly exempt from her wretchedness – in fact, Phyllida was intrigued by the expression in his glittering eyes of a cat anticipating a saucer of cream – but was just as clearly irritated by her adjacent misery and kept darting exasperated glances at her sorrowful profile. She was glad to see Kevin Keithley looking his customary intelligent and balanced self, and resolved to add her approval of his demeanour to the assurances she had been giving Jenny over the past few days that he had not attended the birthday party and had not been picked out by her binoculars on the beach.

'Hello!' he greeted Mrs Sheridan quietly, but with evident pleasure. 'What a ghastly business. I take it you know what's happened?'

'I didn't until Amy called me. As a displaced person I tend not to take in local news. Yes, it's terrible. Have the police–'

'Amy told me when I arrived that they're holding on to the body, so there's no chance yet of a funeral. You may or may not know that the caretaker found the outside door of the theatre unlocked on Friday morning, so at least we aren't forced to suspect one another. There'd been a small select birthday party for Amy on Thursday night, I gather, and Ben had stayed behind when the guests left.'

'On his own?'

'That's one thing everyone seems sure about. Which helps, again.'

'But anyone could have come back,' Sonia ventured.

She and Kevin looked into each other's eyes without expression. 'Exactly,' he murmured eventually. 'Oh, my God. What is it with that boy?'

Phyllida followed his widening eyes to the door. Paul Harper was on his way into the rehearsal room.

The sudden restlessness of those assembling and a series of throat clearings caught Amy's attention, and in a moment she was a whirlwind of rustling polka dots as she tore down off the platform to fold the boy in her arms. Phyllida took his convulsive response to her embrace as a possible explanation for his presence: his caring parents might find it difficult to express their concern and affection.

'Oh, Paul. Oh, my dear boy, we're so dreadfully, dreadfully sorry!'

Amy's unstudied action seemed to dissolve the embarrassment of everyone else, and there was a sympathetic chorus and a sudden general discussion of the topic which Phyllida could tell had so far been carefully avoided. Mrs Sheridan strolled across to the solitary figure of Miss Jones, standing watching.

'What a tragedy!' the American clichéd.

'Yes.' Miss Jones scarcely took her eyes off their survey of the room. She had evidently dismissed the likelihood, once and for all, of

Sonia Sheridan being of any significance in her investigation.

'I gather that poor boy was a great friend of the dead man.'

'I believe so, yes.'

'I must say, I'm a tad surprised that the play's going ahead. And without any delay.'

'I suspect our author has made the point that the dead man wasn't in it.'

Phyllida's instinct, after she had absorbed her surprise, was to congratulate Miss Jones on her wry perspicacity, but she was not keen for the detective sergeant to be made aware of her own and Sonia Sheridan's sense of irony. 'I suppose that's possible,' was all she responded, keeping her amusement out of Sonia's voice. 'But as Miss Tate said to me on the telephone, if they don't keep going now, they'll close for ever.'

'Could be. A-h-h.' DS Jones exhaled a long breath. 'I don't believe it.'

She spoke softly, as if to herself, and again Phyllida's eyes followed another pair of eyes to the door. Now it was Carol Swain who was appearing. Carol Swain, potential heroine of *Interrelations*, whose casting the author had been as delighted with as the casting of Sonia Sheridan and June Jones. It had to be courageous altruism, Phyllida thought. Coupled, perhaps, with a fear of being alone with time to think.

Amy had turned her attention to the latest arrival and was embracing her also, but with less spontaneity. Carol responded with a return squeeze, although compared with Paul's her performance looked dutiful. Phyllida was shocked by her appearance: she was very pale, and there was a twitch at work under one of the eyes that gazed past Amy into space and looked huge in a face which seemed to have lost flesh.

'Oh, my dear,' Amy said, on a gulping breath. 'How positively noble!'

When he saw Carol at the door Henry Hutton had begun a descent from the platform, and he now appeared beside her and put a limp hand on her arm. 'My dear girl. Could this mean...? No. How can I so much as think of it?'

'Yes, Henry, I'll play Clara. What would I be doing at home – sitting alone mourning Ben?'

'I am moved, Carol.' Henry blinked, and Phyllida believed him. Not by other human beings, of course, only by the way they influenced the things he wanted. 'I was about to inform the cast that we must seek another Clara, and that it would be a mountainous task to find one. But now... Thank you, my dear.'

Carol nodded, then moved draggingly over to the front row of chairs where Paul was already sprawled, and sat down beside him. They looked at each other in silence for a moment, and then Paul said 'I'm sorry,' gruffly.

'Thanks. It's bad for you, too,' Carol said, and put her hand lightly on both of his where they were clenched in his lap. She withdrew it quickly, Paul made no attempt to respond to it, and looking at the rigid profiles they had immediately turned to one another, Phyllida had the bizarre fancy that they could be suspecting each other of the murder of the man they had both loved. Looking up at the platform, she saw that Amy and Henry were back in place beside Clive and that all three were watching the two bereaved, Amy with anxious affection, Clive with his usual expression of slight outrage, and Henry with what looked like intense, almost gloating, interest.

Could Henry have come back to the Little Theatre on Thursday night to settle a score? He was the only member of the Company Phyllida could envisage in the role of killer.

Henry was on his feet, welcoming his cast

and thanking them for being there in defiance of the shocking act of violence that had taken place and which they all deplored. 'Ben was a valued member of our team, we shall miss him. Let us now stand in silence for a moment, and remember him.' The old rogue, Phyllida thought. Doing exactly what's right because it isn't costing him a pang and he can be objective. But she was not paid by Peter, she reminded herself, to have opinions with no basis in fact. So far, she had seen and heard nothing that she could offer to Chief Superintendent Kendrick.

'And now,' Henry was resuming, 'let us assemble our players for Act One, Scene One. Those playing Mr Blaketon, Mr Parkinson, Mrs Castlereagh, Sir Arthur. If you'll step up on to the platform... Thank you! We'll work out your positions *vis-à-vis* one another, speak the opening dialogue. Then if we feel comfortable, we'll transfer at our next rehearsal to the theatre stage.' A slight colour had come into Henry's papery skin and his voice held some animation. Amy was not in the first scene, and Phyllida was aware of his impatience as Clive Simpson helped her to her feet and down the steps at the side of the stage. They left the chairs in a row, and with a pettish gesture that involved feet as well as hands, Henry broke it up and was rearranging them roughly in a circle as Carol, after acknowledging Amy's passing hand on her arm with a tortured little smile, climbed the steps.

'Now,' Henry said, after appraising the chairs and his cast, and nodding. 'If Mrs Castlereagh will stand over here...'

'It wasn't a happy first rehearsal,' Miss Bowden told Chief Superintendent Kendrick the next morning. 'Nothing I can say specifically–' Phyllida saw the rueful twitch at the corner of his tense mouth – 'just, really, that no one apart from the author-producer had their heart in it.'

Phyllida had been so disappointed to see the Agency windows in darkness when her taxi deposited her outside the Golden Lion at the end of the rehearsal that she had forced an inward laugh at herself as Mrs Sheridan entered the hotel and went up to Reception.

She had been rewarded. Linda told her Dr Piper had rung just ten minutes earlier and hoped she would ring him back at his home, either from the Golden Lion or when she got home herself. She punched out his number, of course, as soon as she got upstairs, in the moment of kicking off Sonia's elegant shoes.

He answered swiftly and apologetically. 'I've had a visitor tonight, but I'd still have come back to the office for a chat if I hadn't had Kendrick on earlier. He wants us to go see him at ten tomorrow morning, so that you can tell him about your evening at the theatre. Was it really a rehearsal?'

'Oh, yes. Amy said that if they didn't go ahead they'd be finished, and I think everyone was afraid she could be right. And I don't think Henry saw any reason for delay.'

'*I* think you should try not to sound anti-Henry when you speak to Kendrick.'

'Sorry. You're right.'

'Only facts,' Peter advised, apologetic again, as he tended to be when he had successfully offered a rebuke.

'Of course. I'm afraid there are very few of them.'

'Nothing that could be called a revelation?'

'No.'

'Then I'll contain my impatience, and listen with Kendrick in the morning. You're all right?'

'Apart from being affected by the dazed unhappiness of the Little Theatre Company, I'm fine.'

'Somebody could be faking it. They're all used to putting on a show.' Peter paused. 'I suppose if Kendrick actually *asks* you for an opinion as opposed to a fact, you'll have to give it to him.'

'I'll wait for a lead, don't worry. You're all right? You've had a good evening?'

'So-so.' Phyllida wondered if yet another likely girl had turned out to be less so than this unlucky optimist had hoped. 'I'm all right though. Yes.'

'Good. Miss Bowden will be across the Square at half-past nine. I'll stay the night at the hotel, Peter.' Where it would be easier than at home to escape the mood of the evening by ringing down for Scotch and soda and switching on some distractive TV from her bed.

Having already met Miss Bowden, Kendrick was considerably more relaxed for her second visit. He was prepared for his frustration that she had so little to tell him, having learned an hour earlier from DS Jones that the evening at the Little Theatre had offered no revelations.

With the edge off his attention, he found himself wondering why, in an age of a myriad available aids to good looks, a woman whose features really weren't bad should fail to take advantage of any of them. It was a form of arrogance. Unless, of course, Peter Piper really did have only one female field operator and this manifestation of her was, in fact, as complex as all the others.

Kendrick pulled himself irritably out of yet more fruitless speculation about Piper's women. At least they had all proved themselves intelligent, and he had more than once in the past benefited from their opinions even when they had been unable to offer him facts. 'I gather both Paul Harper and Carol Swain turned up last night.'

'Yes. Everyone seemed surprised. Paul Harper isn't in the play, but judging by the way he responded to Miss Tate's embrace, he came for comfort. Carol Swain apparently came so as not to let them down: she was cast as the young lead.'

'You say apparently.'

Phyllida answered swiftly, with a glance at Peter. 'Only because I thought she could have a less altruistic motive as well. Anyone who has just been brutally bereaved might

241

prefer the company of friends and colleagues to being alone.'

'Quite so. How were the two bereaved with one another?'

'Restrained.' Phyllida paused before going on. 'I thought they were wary.'

'As if each might be suspecting the other of the crime?'

'It crossed my mind.' Phyllida's eyes met Peter's expressionlessly.

'Um.' Kendrick wished Miss Bowden didn't have such an unattractive voice. But what she was saying, he admitted to himself grudgingly, was interesting and could be relevant to his inquiry. He was interested, too, by the contrast between her report and that of DS Jones, which had contained no speculation based on her observation of how the suspects interreacted, even when Kendrick had invited it. He wasn't quite sure whether this illustrated a gap in police training – what would he have seen, if he had attended that rehearsal? – or simply DS Jones's personal limitations.

'Did you read anything else from how the birthday party guests behaved and interreacted?' Usually Kendrick found it difficult to ask Piper's women for more than facts, but his question had come on a reflex,

242

making him decide, with relief, that it was DS Jones, rather than the police force as a whole, who lacked a dimension.

'I read an apparent sorrow in Amy Tate, even though she was troupering away. Carol Swain and Paul Harper looked conventionally grief-stricken. Clive Simpson is like Henry Hutton in one way: he doesn't have facial expressions. Though having said that, Henry did show a bit of animation as the rehearsal got under way. He has to have been totally absorbed, because otherwise he would have been affected by the general melancholy. He wasn't – except to get exasperated when his players let their own emotions obtrude on the emotions they were supposed to be portraying.'

'Thank you, Miss Bowden.' To his annoyance, Kendrick found himself wistful that he wasn't hearing this report in the mature American's husky tones, and enjoying her cool elegance. For a shameful moment he even tried to think of a reason for assembling the cast of *Interrelations* so that he could see her again. At least he so angered himself by this display of stupidity that he was able to dismiss all thoughts of the woman he could not – at that moment, at any rate – envisage as Miss Bowden's alter ego. 'Is there anything else you can tell me?' he asked, hearing the question with amazement: despite months of intermittent co-operation with Piper's women, he still had surreal moments when he could scarcely believe he was raking the corners of their minds in the pursuit of his profession. 'Any other – perhaps unlikely – reactions you were aware of?'

'I think Miss Tate was either genuinely very sad, or else she's a brilliant actress. I actually felt she was genuine. But I think I should just say here, Chief Superintendent–' Miss Bowden stirred primly on her chair – 'that although I know I'm a good observer, I've no reason to believe I'm an especially reliable interpreter of what I see.'

'I should say she has got reason, actually,' Peter offered. 'There've been a number of times while Miss Bowden's been working for me that her instincts have proved to be right.' He paused, wondering how to phrase it. 'I think you've seen that for yourself, Chief Superintendent, once or twice when we've been able to assist you.'

'Yes.' The American, the little old lady, the charwoman, the females Piper called Miss Bowden; all had had sound instincts, Kendrick had to acknowledge it. 'That's why I'm asking this kind of question.'

Phyllida hoped for DS Jones's sake that the Chief Superintendent had not found her report too disappointing. 'The only other thing I can say at the moment is that everyone seems to have genuinely liked Ben Carson.' *At the moment.* She mustn't appear to be taking Kendrick's patronage for granted. 'Do you want me to carry on as Sonia Sheridan?'

Kendrick carried out a lightning mental reconnaissance of the current situation: Carol Swain had spent the night of her lover's murder with her mother, leaving the theatre before he did on the evidence of everyone else who had been present. There was no way of checking that Amy Tate, Henry Hutton, and Clive and Angela Simpson had gone straight home and stayed there. The haft of the murder weapon had been wiped clean of fingerprints. There had not been enough blood for stained footprints. Anyone in the world could have entered the unlocked theatre. And DS Jones could deliver only facts.

'For the time being, if you and Mr Piper are willing,' Kendrick reluctantly responded.

# Thirteen

'It's all right for you! It's all right for *you!*' The repeated rebuke ended on an indignant squawk.

'You know, I think it is, Sammy.' Henry Hutton inclined a shoulder and the grey parrot sidled on to it and started gently pecking at his ear. 'I really think it is.'

They were in Henry's kitchen, and Sammy had just walked off the second, and more workmanlike, of his two perches. The ornate one was in what Henry called the drawing room, a large but gloomy north-facing space at the front of the house that looked on to the shrubbery so effectively masking the busy road beyond the red-brick boundary wall. Although Henry was impressed by his drawing room every time he walked into it – it housed the few unsold pictures and pieces of antique furniture collected by his father – when he was at home he tended to spend most of his daylight hours in the big old-fashioned kitchen which faced south and had been the original kitchen before the house had been divided into flats. His drawing room, too, had been the original drawing room and retained the high mantel Henry found so satisfyingly reminiscent of Tenniel's drawing of Alice on her way through the heavy looking-glass above it. At one time he had contemplated reproducing the felt mantel cloth with hanging bobbles prominent in the drawing – his mother had told him when he was a boy that such a cloth, in green, had once hung on that very mantel shelf – but had decided it would be a little too precious a gesture even for one who cultivated preciosity.

It had been a hard decision to split the house up and confine himself to its ground floor, but money had become so tight that the only alternative had been to leave, and after fifty-five years behind that slow-growing shrubbery this was unthinkable. So Henry had ordered the conversion of the three floors into three flats – the upper two with their own outer doors knocked as inconspicuously as possible into hidden angles of the building to enable him to retain the original entrance hall as his sole province. This included the curved staircase, the most elegant feature of the house, which had been cut off out of sight of the hall where it reached the landing, now part of the first-floor flat. It had been a costly undertaking, and by the time the two upper flats were ready for sale the market had moved in favour of the buyer. All Henry had gained from the sacrifice of a large part of his lifestyle had been the precarious possibility of continuing to live at The Laurels with the demeaning prefix to his address of '1'.

Henry's father's profession had been given on the birth certificate of his only child as 'gentleman' and this had turned out to be accurate: Hutton senior had done nothing to maintain or increase the moderate inheritance from his own diligent father beyond dallying inexpertly in the stock market, and had left very little for his wife and son. During her husband's lifetime Henry's mother had been kept in ignorance of her true situation, and had indoctrinated her son with the belief that he would be following in his father's passive footsteps. Hutton senior had died when Henry was seventeen, had just left school with two A levels in history and English literature and was about to set out on the twentieth-century version of a Grand Tour. This had had to be summarily cancelled, and within a couple of months of his father's death Henry had become a junior teller in a Seaminster bank.

The only way to bear it, from the start, had been a rigid separation of his life into two parts. His mother, at first, used timidly to suggest that if he really found his working life as degrading as he was constantly telling her, both his brains and his qualifications could secure him a career in teaching – adult classes or private tutoring, if he didn't want to face the rigours of controlling classes of children who had no wish to learn. But her early washing of those brains had rendered her son far too indolent to stretch them in any way requiring energy and application for something that did not excite him. For forty years Henry had cruised along at various south coast branches of the bank, giving mild satisfaction, and lived at home as his father's son. Had it been available when he was young, he might perhaps have been interested enough through his enjoyment of the theatre to have taken a university course in drama, but that had not then been an option. Unknown to his mother, he had attended various professional auditions for the stage in and out of London, but had failed in all of them. At least, though, he had been able to bestride the amateur stage, and the manner he had so carefully cultivated over the years, when not at the bank, had secured him good and dignified parts and directorial roles. He had been in his forties when he realised that he also wanted to write plays, and one of the two high points of his life was when a well-known publisher of plays for amateurs accepted two of them. The other high point was his retirement from banking.

His mother had managed to remain proud of him, and they had lived amicably enough together for the rest of her life. His retention of his father's old Bentley had been another essential element in the preservation of Henry's *amour propre,* and he had driven his mother from time to time on short sorties inland and along the coast, using public transport or occasionally taxis for most other outings because the Bentley gave him so few miles per gallon of petrol.

Henry's mother had never given anyone any trouble, and had even died, obligingly, while still in possession of her faculties. Nothing much changed thereafter, except that it became easier for Henry to indulge his very private appetite for the intimate company of young men.

He had first recognised that appetite at an early age, when a schoolfellow with whom he had been spending a week of the summer holidays had taken him along to a conclave of naturists to which his whole family belonged. The membership comprised males and females in all shapes and sizes and of all ages, and Henry had been dazzled by the finer specimens of his own sex. The impact of that sunny afternoon had never left him, and as soon as he was old enough to be independent Henry had sought out another such group nearer home, and become a member. The group had been short-lived, as had subsequent groups he had discovered and joined, but he had always managed to find another, and it was at his latest that he had met Ben Carson and Carol Swain. He had in fact been present at the birth of their romance, and had so impressed them with his tales of playwriting and directing that they had auditioned successfully for the Little Theatre Company and transferred there from the amateur society of which at the time they were members. Unfortunately for Henry, his powers of persuasion had worked, too, on a fellow member of that society who was also a member of the naturist group and possessor of the ugliest naked body Henry had ever seen. Although he and Amy Tate had jostled for position ever since, Henry in his innermost heart suspected he was not entirely sorry to have been relieved of the more practical aspects of his chairmanship of the Little Theatre Company. Amy had an eye for quality of writing and performance – he could not otherwise have tolerated her – but was happy to devote her energies to organisation and to leave him to direct the artistic side of things, so that they had gradually developed a grudging admiration of each other's very different strengths.

Over the years Henry's pulling power with young and attractive men had waned, and nowadays, to his abiding pain and distaste, all encounters were dependent on money changing hands, coupled sometimes with the added inducement of one of his ex-quisitely cooked dinners.

When he had left the Little Theatre at the end of Amy's birthday party he had felt rest-less, and desirous of stimulating company. So he had cruised slowly in his unique car (he used it more often these days, ruefully accepting it as more successful than himself in the attraction of punters) and noticed a promising male figure, slight and solitary, leaning on the railings of the Parade and motionlessly contemplating the calm sea.

Henry was realist enough to accept that his fellow thespians probably saw him as an old queen, but he had always striven to keep the facts of his private life entirely to himself and was confident he had managed to do so. His mother had been so totally naive he had felt safe in bringing his prey home to his room from time to time, and he recalled now – with the pang that was the nearest he ever came to affection – her cooing comment one day at breakfast on his kindness to, and encouragement of, young men less gently reared than himself.

He had parked a little way along the Parade to talk to himself and be sure he was lonely enough to risk a rebuff, and when he had decided that he was he retraced his steps by leaving the Parade via one of the small roads leading inland and returning to it via the next, which meant passing the Little Theatre – and seeing someone he knew going in...

'It's all right for *you!*'

Henry beamed on his closest and most intimate friend as the bird repeated the only thing he had ever said. He must have been

253

brought up by a couple where the wife was constantly nagging, Henry had long since decided. He himself could never understand the desire to mate; he had no wish to carry on his unsatisfactory line.

Within twenty-four hours of Ben Carson's death Henry had made a telephone call and suggested a meeting. Even without the corroboration of seeing the killer enter the building where Carson was alone, he would have known who it was: sometimes it seemed to him he was the only person in the Little Theatre Company who had eyes.

As Henry awaited his visitor he reflected, on a quiver of excitement, that this could be the start of a new and profitable undertaking if he were to target younger married men. Pay little to recoup a lot. Money was getting tight again–

The sound of a doorbell broke into his heady reverie. The back doorbell, which was good: he had specified the back door, describing precisely where it was, and the killer was obeying him. Gently easing Sammy back on to his perch, Henry walked across the kitchen to greet his visitor.

'How agreeable to see you! Do please come in!'

The killer obeyed, eyes widening at

Sammy, who had started to dance about his perch and was shouting like an angry woman.

'Excuse me for a moment,' Henry murmured. 'If I give him a titbit he'll quieten down.'

Thinking of Ben Carson's last moments, he felt behind him for the box of Good Boys lying on the work surface, extracted a couple, and held them out to the bird without taking his eyes off the killer. To his surprise Sammy dashed them to the ground and started running up and down his perch, yapping now like a small dog.

Henry cut off his concern as it started: this was not the time.

'Sammy only ever says one thing,' he remarked conversationally, 'but he makes all sorts of uncannily accurate sounds. Now then, to business. You were wise to come – *Sammy!*'

On a piercing scream the bird had left its perch and was flying closely round Henry's head, the brush of its wings stinging his eyes as he struggled to grab hold of it. It had done this before in response to extreme human emotion, perhaps with some avian instinct of offering him protection, and as he tried desperately to catch it Henry tried, too, to damp down his elation in the hope of calming it.

'But you were not wise to invite me,' his visitor said. They were the last words Henry heard.

'It's all right for you! It's all right for *you!*'

Long after the visitor had departed the bird continued in a frenzy, screaming and shouting like a hysterical woman, dancing on its master's chest and tearing at the knife hasp with its bill. The owner of the first floor flat eventually came down his steep narrow stairs and went outside and through the un-locked gate that led into the little yard outside Henry Hutton's back door. The back door was also unlocked but the man didn't try it; he saw enough through the window to tear straight back upstairs and call the police.

Kendrick went in person with DS Wetherhead the moment he was informed, and was admitted via the back door into the kitchen. Even through the gentle hubbub of the forensic and photographic operations he could hear the hoarse screams.

'What in God's name–'

'It's a parrot, sir. It was in here when we arrived, making one hell of a row, if you'll excuse me, sir. It was the parrot that brought the neighbour down from the flat upstairs. When we went through the place we found another perch in the front room, so we – I–' Kendrick noted the bloodstained handkerchief round the uniformed constable's right hand – 'transferred it there. I'm used to handling birds but this is a one-off. It's carrying on like it was the dead man's best friend.'

'Perhaps it was,' Kendrick suggested, recalling Miss Bowden's comments on Henry Hutton.

'Same sort of weapon as the one used on Carson, inserted in the same spot,' DS Wetherhead commented. 'Not that I'm implying the deaths are connected.'

'Of course not, Sergeant. Same sort of improvisation, too.' Kendrick pointed to the gap in the wall-mounted magnetised knife rack.

'Must have been distracted for a moment,' the doctor joined in from the floor, where he was examining the body. 'Doesn't seem on first sight to have resisted. But look at this, Maurice.' Clutched in one of the corpse's hands was a long grey feather.

'It's all right for you! It's all right for *you!*' Both Kendrick and Wetherhead had started in the direction of the hoarse male voice when the wounded uniform moved in front of them and said, 'Parrot.'

'I've got to see this. Lead the way, constable.'

Both men were surprised at the elegant space that lay beyond the kitchen door. The constable led them across it and into a room that was so much darker than the dazzlingly light kitchen Kendrick was guided by his ears rather than his eyes to the shrieking shape that was jumping up and down on a perch near the window.

'It's all right for you! It's all right for *you!*'

The bird fluttered into the air, miaowed, barked, and collapsed back in a heap on the perch, sinking its head between its ruffled feathers.

'At least the row it made must have put the killer off hanging around to look for anything that might incriminate him or her,' Ted said hopefully.

'You're right.' Kendrick's spirits, exhilarated already by the crazy idea that had just exploded inside his head, rose a further notch. 'Come on, Ted.' He led them back to the kitchen at a canter. 'Do the media know anything yet about this murder?'

'No, sir.' The response was unanimous.

'When they *are* let in on it I don't want the parrot around. I want it taken away as a priority to some place of safety, and I don't want *anyone* to know where it's gone. Understood?'

There was another unanimous murmur of assent as the doctor got to his feet. 'What's this all about, Maurice?' he asked curiously.

Kendrick shook his head and tried to smile. 'Nothing, perhaps.' His idea was so wild it probably *would* end up as nothing, but he had to give it a chance. 'Just a thought I've had which depends on that bloody parrot.' He turned to the wounded uniform. 'What's your name, Constable?'

'Woodward, sir. PC Jack Woodward.'

'And you know about parrots?'

'I care about them, sir.'

'Very good, PC Woodward. I entrust the bird and its humane and temporary disposal to you.'

'I could take it home, sir. I live alone. Easy to invent a story to explain its presence.'

'Better and better, constable. Do it. Now. And get it away from this place looking like a cardboard box... There's one other thing I want. From all of you.' Kendrick paused, and one by one the busy team gave him their attention. 'The fact of the parrot's

259

existence is pretty well bound to come out, but I want you to keep to yourselves what you heard it say. You can tell the Press that it mewed and barked and purred, but keep to yourselves the words it used, if you heard them. Have I your undertaking that you'll do that?'

There was a further murmur of assent and a noticeable absence of any exchange of looks, while one or two mouths twitched. Kendrick affected not to notice, and put a restraining hand on his DS's arm as Ted gave a jerk of annoyance.

'Has anyone left the scene yet?'

'No, sir.'

'Good. Anyone know how I get to the flat of the man who found Hutton? What's his name, for a start?'

'John Coombes, sir.' But no one knew the way into John Coombes's flat, and swearing under his breath Kendrick strode towards the back door. 'Come along, Sergeant.'

'I don't understand, sir,' Ted Wetherhead began, as they went outside.

'I'm not sure I do either, Ted, but there's something I want to try. The man didn't go in, he only looked through the window. Odds are Hutton was not in the habit of inviting him in for a drink and a chat. Or any other of his acquaintances. So with luck... And it'll only be for a day or two.'

Round a couple of red-brick angles they found a modest brown door with a brass knocker and a brass '2'. It seemed an age to Kendrick before he heard feet on stairs.

'Yes?' This hall was a tiny lobby, dominated by the young man who faced them and who was almost as tall as Kendrick.

'John Coombes?'

'It is.'

'I'm Chief Superintendent Kendrick and this is DS Wetherhead.' He and Ted held out their warrant cards. 'May we come in?'

'I've been expecting someone, if not someone so elevated.'

The man sounded all right, Kendrick decided, as he ploughed behind him up the steep narrow stairs.

'We shan't keep you long,' he said at the top, trying to disguise the fact, from himself as well as from the others, that he was out of breath. 'We'd just like a statement from you of what you saw – and heard – this morning.'

'Of course. Please sit down.' Coombes waved an arm at the three-piece suite in the centre of what Kendrick thought looked like a one-time master bedroom. He and Ted took the two chairs.

'I heard that wretched parrot shouting and screaming.' Coombes flopped on to the sofa, and Kendrick sensed from his pallor and jerky movements that he was in mild shock. 'That's something I'm always hearing, but not so loud or for so long. The bird sounded so demented and so human I eventually began to wonder if there was something wrong and after I suppose about twenty minutes of the row I went downstairs. I didn't expect Hutton's back gate to be unlocked but I have to pass it on my way to the front of the house so I tried it and it gave. The noise was worse than ever and I ran up to the kitchen window and looked in.' Coombes got up from the sofa and moved over to a side table, where he helped himself to some Scotch with shaking hands. 'I saw Hutton on his back on the floor with the wretched bird dancing about on his chest, and then I saw the handle of a knife sticking out of him. I knew I shouldn't disturb anything so I rushed back upstairs and dialled 999.'

'So you assumed Mr Hutton was dead, sir?' DS Wetherhead inquired.

'He looked it. And ... and perhaps I wanted to think he was, so that I wouldn't feel I ought to go in.' John Coombes stared

262

at the policemen, his eyes widening. 'Oh my God, if he wasn't dead when I saw him, if I could have helped him–'

'The knife thrust killed him instantly,' DS Wetherhead soothed swiftly. 'There was nothing you could have done.'

'Thank God for that.' Coombes hiccuped and buried his face in his hands.

'Did you see much of Mr Hutton?' Kendrick asked him, unable to prolong his respectful silence beyond a few seconds.

Coombes lifted his face, looking slightly better. 'No. I only ever saw him if we happened to coincide in the grounds. If it wasn't for that wretched parrot I wouldn't have known he was there.'

'What about the owner of the flat above you?'

'That flat's empty at the moment. It must have been the last time I saw Hutton, a couple of weeks ago; he was standing beside the For Sale board and groaning. When I asked him what the matter was he told me it offended his sensibilities, he thought it was the last word in vulgarity. I just managed not to tell him I thought he was a damn fool. Oh, God!' Coombes shot to his feet. 'I've nothing against the man, Chief Superintendent. I didn't particularly like him, but

I wouldn't have done him any harm!'

'Sit down, sir,' Kendrick said gently. 'There's no suggestion from anybody that you would. Now, my sergeant has made a note of what you've said, so perhaps you'll be good enough to pop into the station, say tomorrow morning, to read it and sign it if you're satisfied it's what you told us.'

'Yes. Of course.'

'Thank you.' Kendrick got to his feet, and DS Wetherhead followed suit. 'By the way,' Kendrick said casually in the doorway. 'All that shouting and raving and animal noises from Mr Hutton's parrot. Does it ever actually *say* anything?'

'I'm sorry, Chief Superintendent.' John Coombes hauled himself up from the sofa and across the room. 'That view I had of it this morning is the only time I've seen it, so I've no idea.'

'I suppose you'll tell me when you're ready,' Ted said, when they were driving away.

'I'll tell you this afternoon,' Kendrick answered, unable to keep his sense of triumph out of his voice. 'After we've seen Miss Bowden.' He thought it was the first time he had spoken her name without a slight sinking of the heart.

# Fourteen

This time the national media was ready for the word 'Seaminster' and even Mrs Sheridan would have to be aware the following morning that another member of the seaside town's Little Theatre Company had been done to death with a knife.

The second rehearsal of *Interrelations* was due that evening, and Phyllida suggested to Peter that Sonia should telephone Miss Tate. 'The rehearsal's bound to be cancelled, but there could be a shocked get-together in lieu that she could be too shaken up to get round to letting everyone know about and I wouldn't want to miss out on it.'

'Agreed.' But Peter's grin was instantly replaced by a frown in one of the lightning changes that swept so frequently across his expressive face. 'Kendrick,' he said anxiously. 'Are you absolutely sure?'

'Absolutely. Although I'm not so sure I can pull it off.'

'It seems to me a lot of potential danger

for very little potential benefit.'

'That's entirely illogical,' Phyllida said severely. 'If there really is danger, then there really will be benefit. It's as simple as that. And the moment we're aware there's danger, there won't be.'

'There'll be a time lag. A few seconds could be enough. I reckon that was all Carson and Hutton had.'

'I'm going to do it, Peter.'

'It doesn't matter, you know, what Kendrick thinks.'

'I *want* to do it.'

'All right.' Peter got up from his chair with a heavy sigh and moved across to a window. 'If it really is your own decision,' he said with his back to her, 'then I shan't say any more.'

'Thank you. Peter, if there's only one murderer, he or she could be playing ten little Indians, so I'm desperate for that get-together tonight. It'll seem so much less contrived if I can set things up face to face. I'll stay in range of the Golden Lion switch-board this morning and give Amy a chance to make the call first.'

'Why not go home? If she wants to rush round to the hotel and cry on your shoulder you can ask her to postpone it until you're back from wherever you tell her you're just setting out for.'

'All right,' Phyllida said, without enthusiasm.

'When this is over,' Peter said, studying her, 'I'm going to start giving you your own clientele. If the idea appeals to you. Does it?'

'Yes.' Phyllida felt her face transform.

'Good. Just routine stuff at first. There's plenty of it, although I think we've both tended to forget that this past couple of weeks. Now off you go.'

Phyllida was sitting listlessly over the remains of a salad, the latest notes for her book on the arm of her chair, when the telephone rang.

'A Miss Tate,' Sharon told her. 'She asked to speak to you, and when I said you were out she asked when you'd be back. I said I thought it would be fairly soon, and then she said just to leave you the message that–' Sharon paused, and Phyllida's mind's eye saw her picking up the message slip and starting to read – 'the get-together will take place tonight as usual despite what's happened and that she very much hopes you'll be there. She sounded very upset when she said despite what's happened. It's the

267

murder, isn't it? Both murders, I suppose.'

'It is, Sharon. Thanks.'

Phyllida bolted the remains of her salad, put her notes away, collected the drawing and painting equipment she hadn't touched since before *A Policeman's Lot* and drove to a small bay she had discovered a little way east of Billing-on-Sea. It was another fine summer day and there were holidaymakers, of course, on the edge of the sea and spread about the sands, but the bulk of the coast's visitors was divided between the main beaches of Billing and Seaminster, and this sprinkling gave her a choice for the figures in a landscape she would probably have invented if they hadn't been there.

More than two hours passed without Phyllida thinking properly of anything beyond the scene around her and how she could render it with pen and colour wash. When she had resisted the temptation to carry on beyond where her picture was telling her to stop she packed up her equipment and walked for another half-hour barefoot along the edge of the tide, the warm water creaming round her ankles as she tossed a few non-professional thoughts wistfully about her head.

She arrived home refreshed, and eager to

get back to work. It was still several hours before dusk, but cloud across the sun was darkening the fine day and she had already taken so many breaths of sea air she decided to drive into town. She had some pasta and a pot of coffee in her room, and when she had changed she went downstairs and had a drink and a chat with Mick before ordering her taxi, suspecting she was making the most of Sonia's public impact before putting her away that night until her next manifestation. The thought that Phyllida Moon might not be around to put her away slipped only once past her guard.

She should have been expecting it, of course, but it was a jolt to see the jostle of men, women and cameras around the door of the theatre. Kevin Keithley and Clive Simpson were holding them at bay, Clive looking more like an automaton than ever, his expression as unrevealing, his raised right hand as rigid. As she was wrestling her way through she was surprised to see June Jones similarly struggling. Either she was playing Mrs Sheridan's earlier game and pretending ignorance of the second murder, or the professional in Amy Tate, not wanting to lose the Company's other new star, had telephoned her too. Having failed to make the effort Phyllida had made to back up her professional success with some attempt to socialise, DS Jones could not credibly have come to the Little Theatre that night to offer consolation.

'If you could just tell me if you're a member of the Company–'

'Who in your opinion is likely to be the next victim?'

'Are you beginning to think there's a jinx on the Little Theatre Company?'

'Are you in any way connected–'

Mrs Sheridan forged her passage with a smile, Miss Jones hers with a scowl. Kevin and Clive reached out to help them inside before managing to shut and lock the door.

'I think the people we're expecting are here, but if not, the bell rings in the greenroom.' Kevin threw up his arms in a gesture of helplessness. Clive told them gruffly that it was good of them both to have run the gauntlet.

'Miss Tate asked me,' they responded in chorus, and then everyone was silent as they crossed the upstairs foyer to the green room.

Amy, her friend Matty and Carol were leaning against the bar counter, and Angela Simpson was sitting shivering at the table nearest to it. Paul Harper was drooping alone at another table, and other members of the cast of Henry's ill-fated play were standing or sitting around, all motionless as they turned towards the newcomers. Phyllida had a fantasy that she was watching a posed *tableau vivant,* which broke up as Amy Tate came forward to greet them. Like Carol, although in a very different way, she appeared diminished, and reminded Phyllida of a balloon that has just started to deflate.

'Kevin. Sonia,' she said without energy. 'Miss Jones... How good of you. Braving that mob outside. This is so terrible it hardly feels real.'

'It is real, though.' Carol Swain had joined them. 'It has to be, because Ben and Henry aren't here any more.' Where shock had turned Miss Tate rosy and restless, it had rendered Carol Swain pallid and minimal of gesture, more gaunt even than when Phyllida had last seen her, a different woman from the poised blonde who had smiled on the would-be recruits attending the Company's audition such a short time ago.

Paul Harper had got to his feet, and was wandering zombie-like towards the group at the bar counter. 'I wonder which of us it will be next?' he asked, with an uncomfortable little laugh, his eyes staring through them. 'Well, if it's me I shan't mind.'

'Don't talk like that, Paul!' Kevin spoke sharply against a background of audibly intaken breaths and a yelp from Matty. 'I for one shan't be surprised if it comes out that there are all sorts of nasties in Henry's woodshed that have nothing at all to do with the Little Theatre.'

'Thank you, Kevin.' Amy tried to smile. 'But two knifings of two members of the casting committee ... Paul could be right, we have to face it.'

'Two down and three to go,' Paul said.

'For God's sake!' Kevin shouted, and Matty wailed, 'Don't! Oh, don't!'

'If you're really worried you could ask for police protection,' June Jones suggested. 'Although I don't suppose that means you'd automatically get it.' Her beautiful voice must make everything she said sound significant, Phyllida thought wistfully, but what she had said just now was more significant than anyone else present could realise. Phyllida wondered if the suggestion was the detective sergeant's own, or whether she had been ordered to offer a qualified assurance if she saw panic looming.

'I've made coffee,' Carol said, looking at Amy with concern as she took her arm. 'Let's drink it before it goes cold. Come on.'

As she and Kevin were attempting to seat the two large ladies near the coffee table Angela Simpson jumped to her feet and ran across to throw her arms round Amy and tell her chokingly how sorry she was.

Sobbing, Amy returned the hug so generously that for a moment Angela disappeared from sight inside her huge embrace. The scene was so touching Phyllida had to remind herself of Amy's thespian resources ... and the acting ability of the rest of the cast of Henry's play.

Angela Simpson's apparently spontaneous show of concern seemed to help Miss Tate to pull herself together, and when she had taken a couple of deep draughts of coffee, and eaten two biscuits, she got to her feet and moved back to the bar.

'Thank you for coming here tonight,' she said. Even in her distress her voice was so powerful she secured everyone's immediate attention. 'I have to tell you that the casting committee' – 'What remains of it,' Phyllida heard Paul mutter – 'has decided to cancel the production of Henry's new play, a decision I don't think will surprise any of you. We sincerely hope the play will have its premiere in the not too distant future, if not in a production at this theatre. We have also decided for the time being to suspend all our professional and social activities.'

'In the hope, let me explain, that it may make it a bit harder for the murderer to find us.'

'Stop it, Paul!'

This time is was Clive Simpson who rebuked the boy. He had sprung to his feet and was glaring across at him. Phyllida saw that his normally rigid body was trembling from head to foot.

'Yes, please, Paul!' Amy added her plea, uncharacteristically imploring.

June Jones suggested that everyone should try to be calm. She looked so entirely a member of the police force that Phyllida found herself wondering if she was about to produce her warrant card.

Not as preliminary to arrest, though. Her presence in the theatre had to mean that Chief Superintendent Kendrick remained frustratingly in the dark.

'I have something to tell you all,' Mrs Sheridan drawled into the unhappy silence. 'Just this morning I received some news that

makes it necessary for me to leave Seaminster in a day or two's time and go back
home.' Phyllida's glance had been moving
round the attentive circle as she spoke and
was on Kevin as she paused, surprised by
what looked like the shock and disappointment in his eyes. But the reaction
was so unlikely, and was so quickly gone,
she decided she had imagined it. 'Not bad
news, I'm glad to say, but just now the
family needs me.' That should be enough to
discourage questions. 'When I had Amy's
call this afternoon I was trying to get my
courage up to break the news to Henry that
I would have to withdraw from the cast of
*Interrelations*. And now it's academic, and
I'm so very sorry. Thank you all for welcoming me so generously into the Little
Theatre Company. I sincerely hope that the
police will soon make an arrest – arrests
perhaps–' Kendrick didn't even know if
there was one murderer or two – 'and you'll
be able to get back to normal. I'll be the
other side of the Atlantic, but I'll be thinking of you.'

'Thank you, Sonia,' Amy responded
against a background of self-deprecating
murmurs, encircling Phyllida's arm with a
large warm hand. 'It's been a privilege to

have had you with us. Henry thought so, too,' she concluded, with what Phyllida suspected was a slight effort.

'I guess I'll have a coffee now.' Mrs Sheridan made a move towards the coffee pot, but Kevin smiled and shook his head. By the time he had put the coffee on the bar counter in front of her, the talk had subsided into individual chat within small groups, as Phyllida had hoped it would, giving Sonia the best scenario for issuing her invitations.

Kevin had remained beside her, so she began with him. He hadn't been a guest at Amy's birthday party, but she felt she had got to know him better than she had got to know any other member of the Little Theatre Company – which meant, she tried to reassure herself, that it was probably of no real significance if he *was* upset at the prospect of her departure. And everyone who had been in Seaminster the night of Ben Carson's death was his possible assassin, because he had been alone in the theatre with the door to the street unlocked.

'Kevin. Would you be able to join me and a small group of the other friends I've made at the theatre for a farewell drink tomorrow evening? Say six thirty at the Golden Lion, where I'm staying. I do hope you can manage it.'

Kevin was smiling, looking pleased. 'I can indeed. And if I'd had another engagement, I'd have tried my best to put it off.'

'Thank you. I thought we'd meet in the small bar. Do you know it?' He did, because he'd once taken Jenny there.

'Of course. I'll look forward to seeing you there at half-past six tomorrow.'

'My pleasure. Now, I have one or two other invitations to give out. So if you'll excuse me...' Sonia drained her coffee cup and strolled off to find her other would-be guests.

Amy, Matty, Carol and the Simpsons all appeared happy to accept Sonia's invitation for a farewell drink. Even Paul offered a sullen thanks, and Amy undertook to ensure his presence, to the extent of calling for him.

According to the instructions she had received, and her own instincts, Phyllida's duties for the evening were not yet quite done. 'I heard on the radio this morning that Henry had a parrot,' she remarked, as Paul wandered off across the room and Sonia joined Amy, Matty and Carol at the table where they were sitting. 'The neighbour who discovered – the body –

apparently saw it through the window and said it appeared to be very distressed. I've heard that parrots have exceptional brains for birds. Did any of you ever see it?'

'Henry never invited anyone to his house,' Carol said. 'At least–' She glanced at Amy, who shook her head.

'He never invited *me*. I've sometimes wondered who the people were who he invited to his little suppers.'

'His boyfriends, I should imagine,' Carol said.

'Carol! How can you!' Amy's reaction seemed to be a spontaneous mixture of shock and astonishment.

'Oh, come on, Amy! He was brilliantly discreet, I have to admit – I suppose one could just believe he was non-functional in the sexual area – but I'd put my money on him going for the boys. He certainly hadn't the least interest in women apart from their mental and aesthetic qualities as actresses.'

'I think I'd agree with Carol,' Sonia said. 'Although as I've been among you for such a short time I probably shouldn't offer an opinion. But that was the impression Henry Hutton gave me.'

'Ask a man,' Carol suggested. 'Here's Kevin. Kevin, Amy was surprised when I suggested Henry was gay. You'd say I was right, wouldn't you?'

'Oh, yes.' Kevin hadn't hesitated. 'I'm sorry, Amy.'

'You mustn't be sorry,' Carol said. The green-room bar was dry, but from the uncharacteristically careless way she was speaking Phyllida suspected she had been drinking before coming to the theatre. 'And neither must you, Amy. To be sorry would be fearfully politically incorrect. It's always being dinned into us these days that to be gay is simply to be different. Not inferior.'

'I know, I know,' Amy disclaimed quickly, as Kevin shrugged and smiled and Matty clicked her tongue. 'It's just ... When you learn something important about someone you've known for a long time, it takes a bit of adjusting to. If you're right!' she added, with a hint of her old confidence.

'Oh, I'm right,' Carol said indifferently.

'I must go.' Sonia got to her feet. 'I've so much to see to.'

'How did you get here?' Kevin asked. 'Can I give you a lift?'

'I called a taxi. It's good of you, Kevin, but it'll be easy enough to call another.'

'Don't dream of it. I'm ready to go my-self.'

'Well, thank you, then.' It was silly to feel reluctant because of an instant's reaction that might or might not have crossed his eyes.

Phyllida was not sorry to be leaving the Little Theatre green-room for the last time. A goose walked over her grave as she crossed the foyer, and she thought as she shivered how the innocent would now walk in fear, however absurd they might claim aloud it was to be afraid that a person who had killed twice would be bound to kill a third time. To solve the murders could be to save another life. The possibility that she could play a part in the solution was very slender, but it was there, and she must think of it later when she was alone and her own fears began crowding in.

When he drew up outside the Golden Lion Kevin switched off the engine and turned to look at her.

'When did you say you were leaving?' he asked.

'The day after tomorrow.'

'Leaving England then? Or just Seaminster?'

'Leaving England, Kevin. Flying out from Heathrow.'

'Ah. I see.'

He turned away from her on an audible sigh, and Phyllida faced the possibility that Jenny's sedate boyfriend had fallen for an older woman.

But it couldn't be. It mustn't be.

'All good things come to an end,' she said lightly, grateful for the defence of her American voice. 'I'll see you tomorrow evening, Kevin. Thanks for the lift.'

He made a move towards her, but it was only to lean past her to open the passenger door, and when she was on the pavement and she met his eyes she saw that they contained nothing but courtesy.

'Goodnight, Sonia. I look forward to your little party.'

Standing on the steps of the Golden Lion while he drove away, Phyllida had to stifle an hysterical giggle.

It was a further relief to see the light in the second floor windows across the Square. She and Peter had made their plans and she had little as yet to report, but a drink and a chat would postpone her solitude and boost her courage. And she didn't want to laugh alone about her absurd overestimation of Mrs Sheridan's powers of attraction.

# Fifteen

Tables in the small bar at the Golden Lion were not normally reservable, but Mrs Sheridan had no difficulty in securing one, even at the popular hour of six thirty p.m. Several times over the past months, late at night when the windows across the Square were dark, one of Phyllida's women had perched on a stool at the counter and made the odd contribution to Mick the barman's putting of the world to rights. During the day Mick presided over the long bar in the foyer, but in the evening he preferred the smaller, more intimate space patronised by his regular customers and left the outer area to his two subordinates. Usually he made his move at seven, but he was in the small bar to welcome Mrs Sheridan when she came in just before half-past six the following evening, to undertake to do what she asked him, and to indicate the reserved sign on one of the two larger tables that occupied a couple of the cosily under-lit corners; the low lights might inhibit

Phyllida's observation of the reactions of her guests, but they would also soften the intensity of Mrs Sheridan's gaze, and if what she said found its mark, she would be made aware of it later.

Phyllida settled herself in the angle, aware of her heartbeat and wishing she could have ordered herself an immediate drink. But the arrival of her first guest would allow that while still maintaining Mrs Sheridan's invariable good manners, and she tried to distract herself by opening a mental book on who it would be. As Jenny was constantly extolling his good timekeeping she gave Kevin the shortest odds, and he came into the bar while she was still placing the rest of the runners.

Mrs Sheridan willowed to her feet, a hand extended. 'Kevin! So good to see you.' Mick was instantly at the table. 'What would you like to drink?'

Kevin asked for Scotch, and Phyllida ordered her own and Sonia's favourite aperitif.

'Now,' she said, as Kevin seated himself beside her. 'Have you seen Amy or any of her birthday party guests today? It's going to take them a long time to come to terms with what's happened. Especially as for the time being they're losing the outlet which would help them.'

'I know.' Kevin looked instantly grave, and Phyllida realised this was not the first time she had had an instinct that the apparent darkening of his mood was assumed to suit the context rather than a true reflection of how he felt. It was as if his real stance was an impervious detachment from the terrible events afflicting the members of the Little Theatre Company, enabling him to switch on the appearance of shock and horror at will. 'Sonia? You look pensive?'

She had been reflective too long; it was an early warning for which she was grateful. Looking into Kevin's politely concerned face, Phyllida decided she had been led astray by her intense desire to discover that something – anything – to do with these people was not what it seemed.

'I'm sorry.' Reassuringly she smiled at him. 'It's just that ... I wasn't ready to go home. I was – am – enjoying Seaminster and my new friends, and I thought I was going to be able to go on enjoying them for quite some time yet. The closing of the theatre makes it a bit easier to go, maybe, but it also makes me feel I'm walking out on the members and their troubles.'

'That's absurd!' In less solemn vein he seemed far more sincere. 'No one can do anything about events beyond their control, and that's your situation now, isn't it? I'm not trying to pry, Sonia, but I get the feeling that for one reason or another you've no choice but to leave.'

'That's right. But I'm still sad to go. Ah, here comes Mick. We won't be sad this evening.'

'And here are Amy and Paul. And Miss Thompson,' Kevin added, in a less enthusiastic tone, as he got to his feet.

'Welcome!' Sonia said, also rising. 'Don't go away, Mick, without taking further orders.'

Amy asked for a glass of white wine, Paul a lager, and after some discussion it was decided that Matty would do best with a double tomato juice. 'She likes plenty of Worcester sauce,' Amy bawled.

Irresistibly reminded of a comedian and a stooge, Phyllida turned to greet the Simpsons and take their orders while Mick was still within earshot. Clive in drag would be even better than Miss Thompson in the stooge's role, she decided, as she shook the rigid hand and found Sonia's warm smile elicited no response beyond a sharp nod of the head. Angela, on the other hand, leaned up to kiss her cheek. Both asked for wine.

'So how are you, Paul?' Sonia ventured, when they were all seated and she could see that there was still just room at the table for the narrow Carol.

The boy shrugged, then appeared to remember the manners Phyllida had seen from the start that he had been taught. 'Thank you, I'm all right.'

'Have you finished your exams?'

Paul Harper gave a scornful little laugh that consigned his exams to the level of trivia. But he went on to say – hesitantly, as he had said everything since Ben Carson's death – that there was a week's respite before the final couple, and he expected at least to go through the motions.

'Good for you. Now, where's Carol?'

'Probably kept late at the office!' Amy boomed, her laugh sounding particularly large and generous in contrast to Paul's. 'For legitimate reasons, I may say. The poor girl works very hard, and she's the sort who'll turn to work now rather than go off the rails. She has her head screwed on.'

'That's the impression she gives me.' Sonia turned to Matty. 'I'm glad you could join us,' she said. Phyllida herself basked in the generous tone of her American hospitality, and Matty beamed as she thanked Mrs Sheridan for her invitation.

'Sorry, sorry!' Carol was at the table, as immaculately turned out as ever but conveying to Phyllida through her strained smile an impression of inner disarray. 'Something came up, which you can be certain it always will do on the nights you're anxious to get away.' Her voice, weak and slightly hoarse, added to the impression despite the determined flippancy of what it was saying.

'It's good to see you, Carol, and I appreciate very much that you've joined us tonight.' Mick was back beside them. 'What will you drink?' Carol chose Scotch and squeezed into the space between Amy and Kevin.

'Do you really have to leave us?' Amy asked Sonia.

'From conscience, if not from coercion. Family. I'm afraid the ocean has failed to wash out my sense of obligation. But I hope to be back.' Mrs Sheridan smiled round on each of them in turn. 'It's been a great pleasure working with you all, and I shall always regret never having played Mrs Castlereagh.'

'It *is* a disappointment,' Amy said wistfully, before catching Carol's huge sad eyes and floundering hastily into pious expression of nothing mattering compared with the loss of human life.

'It's all right, Amy,' Carol said listlessly. 'Everything's so utterly unbelievable we none of us can quite know what we're saying or doing. Feeling unreal's helping me in a way, but then I suddenly realise I'm not dreaming and I–' Carol stopped speaking abruptly and took a long drink from the glass Mick had just set in front of her.

'If I was involved,' – Matty Thompson made no attempt to disguise her complacency that she was not – 'I'd be scared. Someone who's killed twice could kill a third time. And a fourth. I keep telling Amy she should ask for police protection but she doesn't listen.'

'If there's just one murderer,' Phyllida began slowly, hoping she was going to be able to express for her own reassurance as well as that of her guests the conclusions she, Peter and the Chief Superintendent had attempted to reach the night before, 'then I think he or she will reckon their luck has run out by now. And if there are two – well, Henry's death could well have had nothing to do with the Little Theatre Company.' But there were two opportune knives, and the three detectives had eventually come down on the side of a single killer. 'I know it's all very well for me to say not to worry, not being involved, like Matty.' Phyllida tried to keep the irony out of her smile. 'But I think what I've just said makes sense.'

'I think so, too,' Clive pronounced, at the end of a short contemplative silence all round. It was the first time Phyllida had heard him pass an opinion. 'But I also think we should leave it to the police to work things out.'

'Or we'll start wondering about one another and poisoning our friendships,' Kevin contributed.

'You're both right.' She must change the subject, lull the guilty – if he or she was at the table – into a sense of security until her final comment. 'So let me enjoy my last moments with you–' Phyllida wished she had said that another way – 'and carry away a memory of the good people and good things Seaminster has given me. D'you know, I suddenly felt inspired the other day and I took a taxi out to a little bay I discovered a while back beyond Billing. I always carry a small pack of watercolour paints and pencils with me when I travel, in the hope I may want to use them sometime. I asked the driver to come back in an hour's time, and when he did I was so caught up I sent him away for another hour, and managed a bit of a wade as well before he came back again.'

Phyllida was glad to see the relieved smiles. Angela asked her if she was a good artist.

'Competent. Nothing out of the ordinary. And I've been too nomadic lately to manage much, so I was tentative at first. But by the time I packed up I felt it had begun to come back.'

'Skills properly learned do come back,' Amy pronounced. 'I was very rusty with my French when I went to Paris last year after not going for ages, but by the time I came home I was rattling on again.'

'I can't draw a straight line!' Matty announced proudly.

Phyllida managed to keep it like that through two rounds of drinks, even drawing Paul out to talk for a few moments about his taste in music.

When most glasses were empty for the second time, Kevin thanked Sonia for an interlude he hoped had made everyone feel better, and said it was time to break the party up and let her get on with her preparations for departure. The others murmured their agreement and Sonia, Phyllida's heart almost deafening her, said how much she had enjoyed being with them all.

'For the last time,' she added, with a regretful smile at each in turn. 'Oh, just before we go our ways – there's a phrase that's been going round in my head for the past couple of days and it's driving me crazy. You know the way you suddenly find yourself singing a few notes of a tune? Well, with me this time it's a few words. I must have picked them up from the radio or TV, I suppose, somebody's catchphrase.'

Phyllida paused, and Matty asked her what it was.

'"It's all right for you! It's all right for *you!*" I can even hear the tone of voice, very harsh and the second time quite angry. *Is* it some comedian's catchphrase? Can one of you put me out of my misery?'

Again Mrs Sheridan turned her lazy gaze through the circle of her guests. Paul had his eyes on the table and was shaking his head. Amy and Matty were looking at each other, then shaking theirs, too, before turning to look at their host and saying sorry with what looked like puzzled faces. Angela Simpson looked puzzled as well, but her husband as usual showed no reaction, beyond glancing at his watch. Carol and Kevin were both politely smiling.

'Sorry,' Carol said. 'But I don't have much time to watch TV and I just have news or music on the radio.'

'I'm sorry too, Sonia,' Kevin said. 'It sounds like a nagging wife in some TV sitcom, but I hardly ever watch them and I've certainly not heard it anywhere else.'

'I can't help, either.' Angela Simpson turned to her husband. 'Can you, Clive?' Clive Simpson shook his head. 'Sorry, Sonia.'

'Never mind. These things don't usually last long.'

They were all on their feet now, all looking guestly and grateful and unshaken, and Phyllida rose to join them, not knowing if she was disappointed or relieved but telling herself that she had merely set the trap and it was too early to be either. Whoever had killed had proved the strength of their nerve before tonight, and if they were at the table would be able to hide their reaction. And if she was surrounded by the innocent, then nothing would happen and their innocence would be nearer to being proven.

Mick was beside her. 'Anything else I can get you?' he asked.

Phyllida looked questioningly at a succession of shaken heads. 'It seems not, Mick, thanks.'

'Room 36 isn't it, Mrs Sheridan?'

'That's right.' Sonia signed the chit.

'When exactly are you leaving?' Amy asked, as Mick went back to the bar.

'Lunchtime tomorrow. I fly to New York from Heathrow in the late afternoon. So – goodbye. Good luck. And thank you for making me so welcome.'

'We'll miss your acting skills,' Amy said wistfully. 'When we reopen the theatre. Which we will.'

'We will!' was the chorus, and then they had all walked out to the foyer and she had seen them threading through the swing doors.

Phyllida went back into the small bar to thank Mick, then nodded to the two girls in Reception and went slowly up the main staircase. This time when she reached the first floor she turned a different way, unlocked a door in the wide corridor, and entered one of the Golden Lion's most

293

splendid rooms. An internal door connecting it with the next room was open, and as Phyllida closed the outer door behind her two men in plain clothes came through to greet her.

'Everything go as planned, Miss Bowden?' one of them asked.

'Yes. But nothing given away. We could be in for an uneventful night.'

Both men grinned. 'It's pretty comfortable in there.'

'That's nice for you. Is everything ready?'

'Yes. Down to our supper tray.'

'Good. I'm about to order mine. As everything's ready I think we should close and lock the door. If somebody's going to visit me I've a feeling they won't waste much time. Now, I know that any visitor I may have tonight won't see Mrs Sheridan as on the side of the law, and that if they look for anything it won't be for more than a recording device set up to ensure her personal safety. But could he or she mistake *your* devices for that, and damage or dismantle them?'

'We've been working here most of the day,' the other one said. 'You'll be all right.'

When she had heard the key turn the far side of the door into the next room Phyllida

went to the telephone and ordered sandwiches and coffee. 'Right away, if you will.'

She had to worry the sandwiches down,
but she was glad of the coffee. And despite
the acrobatics being performed by her
heart, as she looked round the room she had
to smile at one of the most authentic-look-
ing stage sets she had ever occupied. Almost
the whole of the wardrobe belonging to Mrs
Sheridan and her other manifestations was
strewn about and there was a suitcase open
on the bed lined with elegant underwear.
Miss Bowden's professional ID was next
door with the detectives in Phyllida's working bag, and in the thin top drawer of the
bedside table in the room where she was
waiting there reposed a US passport
carrying Mrs Sheridan's photograph and
physical details. Phyllida imagined the Chief
Superintendent agonising over how
thorough to make his charade, and the
amount of skill and working time he could
justifiably give to what, if it failed, could all
too easily be viewed by the Chief Constable
of Seaminster as an extravagant caprice
unworthy of a very senior policeman.

Her own reasoning told her it would be
enough for the visitor she might receive to
be aware that the woman occupying Room

36 at the Golden Lion hotel shared Henry Hutton's knowledge about the first murder and had drawn her conclusions about the second; whether Mrs Sheridan was who she claimed to be would be irrelevant. But once Kendrick had embarked on his eccentric enterprise, he had identified more and more areas in which he felt it must present an appearance of authenticity.

She and Peter had joined him in reasoning that she was unlikely to be in physical danger from whoever came to visit Mrs Sheridan, if only because it would be obvious to the killer that she would not have invited a private meeting without taking precautions for her personal safety. They had also reasoned that the killer would assume that Sonia Sheridan, revealing herself as Henry Hutton's accomplice or at least his friend, already knew who he or she was and would therefore see nothing to lose by accepting an oblique invitation from a woman who could be no keener than him or herself to get involved with the police.

Good reasoning, Phyllida told herself, as she forced down the last of the sandwiches and starting pacing the room, coffee cup in hand. Reasoning which continued to hold up as she went through it all again. But

which was not proof, she steadily discovered, against the panic seizing her more
and more strongly as she stared at the stout
locked door separating her from her
protectors. Despite all the precautions, all
the reassurances, she knew that, if the
person who visited her was crazy, none of
the logic of the situation would save her
from death.

When seven o'clock had taken several
hours to become eight o'clock, Phyllida
decided to switch off the television she had
been trying to watch in favour of trying to
read a book. Her outer door was the far side
of a small lobby, and although her hearing
was acute and she had kept the TV sound
low, she found herself beginning to worry
that she might not hear a tap at the door.
Dismissing – not without difficulty – the idea
of moving a chair into the lobby, she settled
into the one nearest to it and opened the
crime novel she had begun earlier which
assured its readers via the blurb that it would
transport them into another, more thrilling,
world. It was not the author's fault, Phyllida
reflected, as she tried to remember what she
had already read, that the world she was in
was providing excitement enough.

She was amazed, when the knock came, to

find it had woken her out of a doze. But the zombie she had become was instantly awake and alert, moving swiftly across the dimly lit lobby, unlocking the door, grasping the knob, turning it and pulling the door towards her.

Standing close against it was a bulky figure wearing an anorak and an unbecoming woolly hat pulled down to eye level. The lower part of the face was hidden too, by a thick scarf, but the overall shape was un-mistakeable.

*Amy.*

*Oh, I didn't want it to be you!*

As disappointment flooded through her fear, Phyllida realised she had come to believe that Amy Tate was a good woman.

## Sixteen

'Come in.' Phyllida stood aside for the ungainly figure to precede her through the lobby, and shut the door on to the corridor before following it into the room. 'You're dressed for winter. I suppose it's a disguise.'

'Oh, yes. It's a disguise.'

The voice, and the bitter little laugh, told Phyllida there was something wrong before the clothes began to join Mrs Sheridan's on the bed. The anorak, the scarf, the hat, a pillow, another pillow...

Carol Swain was standing there, wanly smiling.

'Your reaction's telling me it was an effective disguise.'

'It was. Even though I was expecting you.' The essential lie, and Phyllida thanked fate that she had not said Amy's name.

'May I sit down?'

Phyllida nodded, watched the girl drop into one of the room's two armchairs, and sat down in the other. She found she was having no difficulty accepting Carol as the killer, even though she looked the way she had looked a few hours ago in the bar downstairs: strained, sad, exhausted.

'I didn't know Henry had a partner in crime,' Carol said, leaning back with a sigh. 'You really are a good actress. I suppose you've asked me here because you want to carry on where I made him break off?'

The voice was flat, defeated, and the eyes that stared across the room into Phyllida's held neither fear nor anger.

'No. I just want to know why you killed

him. And the man you told me one night not long ago that you loved – so much.'

'Loved to death. Wasn't that what you were going to say? It turned out to be true.'

'But why, Carol?'

Carol Swain got to her feet and started walking about the room. Even when she passed behind Phyllida's chair Phyllida found she had no fear of her.

'Because he fell in love with Paul Harper. Gave in to what he told me the night I killed him that he'd been struggling against for years. I had no idea, not the least suspicion. When he didn't feel like making love, which I tried not to believe was more and more often, I accepted his excuse that he was tired.' The bitter little laugh again. 'But it was because he preferred to make love to Paul. To other men.' This time it was a sob. 'When we were on the beach that night there was something ... I'm classically inclined as an architect and I've seen a lot of depictions of male Greeks at play. And you know what *that* meant... I saw them running together, I saw the way Paul looked at Ben, and I wondered if Paul... Not Ben, that never crossed my mind. Only Paul.' Carol paused, on another sob. 'It would have explained why he's changed. I wanted to speak to Ben, to find out if I was right. If Paul... Ben had brought him to the beach – I'd come under my own steam – so of course Ben was taking him home. I asked him to come to me for the night afterwards, but guess what, he said he was tired.' Carol flung herself back into her chair. 'We were both working late the next day, and Amy's party was under way when we arrived – separately again, as it was straight from work for both of us. When we'd managed to get together out of earshot of other people I asked Ben if he'd stay behind after the party so that we could have a word. My mother was expecting me and I couldn't get there too late, so it seemed the only opportunity and all day I'd somehow been needing more and more to ask him about Paul. Ben said he wanted a word with me, too, and we agreed that I'd leave early, shoot home to get something for my mother I'd forgotten to bring with me, then go back to the theatre when the others had left – he'd tell them he'd lock up. If the cars were still in the car park I was going to put mine round the corner – there seemed no point in making people wonder what I was doing coming back to the theatre after saying I was on my way to Brighton – but by the time I got back they'd all gone so I parked in the theatre car park. Could I have a drink?'

'Surely. Scotch?'

Carol nodded and Phyllida got up, poured her a measure, and put it on the table beside her chair with the jug of water that was regularly renewed in every Golden Lion bedroom.

'Thanks.' Carol took a drink without diluting it. 'I found Ben in the green-room and I asked him right away if he was having trouble with Paul, and he said no, and then he told me... He'd faced the fact that he was gay, and that was the way he was going to live from now on. And then he said he still loved me.' She was on her feet again and flinging about the room. 'Perhaps it was that – that insult – that sent me mad, I don't know. But just for a moment the thought of what he'd done with Paul – what he'd do with him again – with other men... We were facing each other at the bar counter and the knife was by my hand. It was like my hand grabbed it and I went at him before my mind knew what I was doing. He backed against the counter, which made it easy to push the knife in. I don't know anything about anatomy, but I must have found his heart. Just for a moment, when I saw him fall, I was glad about what I'd done, I felt I'd prevented something much more terrible, and I was able to wipe the knife up to where it had gone into him. But afterwards, right away afterwards, while I was looking down at his eyes that couldn't see me, I'd have done anything in the world to turn the clock back. Oh, God...' Carol sank down in her chair and closed her own eyes, and Phyllida saw the tears squeezing under her lashes as she waited in silence.

'Since then nothing's mattered,' Carol said eventually, sitting up and blinking. 'I felt dead myself. When Henry rang and told me he knew what was going on between Ben and Paul – it takes one to know one, I suppose – and that he'd seen me going back into the theatre and would like a chat, it didn't seem important. When I went to see him I'd no thoughts of killing him, I didn't even know whether or not I was going to agree to pay him the money it was obvious he would be asking me for. It didn't seem to matter one way or the other, I didn't care what happened to me, my life was over.' Carol leaned forward in her chair and stared into Phyllida's eyes. 'I might make sure soon that it really is, but I'm glad to be talking about it. It's so heavy on my own.

'I suppose if you've done it once... Henry told me I'd been wise to go and see him, and that made me feel angry – the only feeling I'd had since I'd killed Ben – but it was only when that parrot started trying to protect him and I saw the knives on the wall that I thought of killing him. But I didn't think of killing him!' Carol was suddenly shouting. 'I just did it! His arms were up trying to catch the parrot and his chest was exposed – he was wearing a T-shirt with some ridiculous slogan on it about saving the planet – and I grabbed the knife and ... I'd killed someone else. Even if the parrot hadn't been making such a row I doubt I'd have stayed around to look for anything that might have incriminated me because I didn't care, it didn't matter whether or not they caught me. I wiped the handle of the knife on a reflex before just walking out the way I'd walked in and getting back into my car and driving away. I've done everything on a reflex since then, talking, eating, working. When you quoted the parrot tonight it was like a relief, like an unburdening in advance of what I knew after you'd spoken I was going to tell you.'

So the little smile had been Carol's real reaction.

'And then kill me, too?'

Carol smiled again. 'No.' She looked at Sonia as if she had shut off her inward visions and was really seeing her for the first time since she had entered her room. 'Not just because you're bound to have protected yourself some way. You have, haven't you?' she asked, idly curious. 'Or you wouldn't have invited me.'

'Oh, yes. I've protected myself. But tell me, Carol.' Phyllida leaned forward in her turn. 'Is there anything that could happen that could make you feel better, make you feel you might still have some life left?'

'I'll never feel better,' Carol said flatly. 'But if I could pay for it–'

'You could turn yourself in.'

Another smile. 'I know. I've thought about it. Over and over. But I can't. It's not cowardice, because as I've told you I don't care what happens to me and maybe the tougher the better. I suppose it's that I don't want to admit to the world that I killed the only person I've ever really loved.'

'I'm afraid you *have* admitted it, Carol.'

'You mean you're going to turn me in?' There was a brief leap of alarm in Carol's eyes before she shrugged and sank back in her chair.

'I mean you've turned yourself in.' Phyllida got to her feet and went over to the connecting door. 'And you've also told the world you'd give your life to turn the clock back.'

The door opened as Phyllida raised her hand to knock.

It was past midnight, and events had torn Chief Superintendent Kendrick from his hearth and home and brought him back to the office, but he had listened to the recording of the conversation between Carol Swain and Miss Bowden and was full of cheer. To the rare, delightful extent of knowing it, of being able to say in his head 'This is happening *now;* I am tasting satisfaction in this instant.' He was aware, of course, that not everything was as yet signed and sealed, but the sensation of it all coming together was so strong in him he had to abort a smile when a knock came at his door.

It was DS Wetherhead, with a smile that made Kendrick reinstate his own. 'Sorry to bring you in at this ungodly hour, Ted, but it all seems to be happening. Piper's woman has come up trumps unscathed.' His chief – unexpressed – worry over his mad parrot idea had been that despite all precautions the unexpected could have wiped out a percentage, if not all, of Piper's female field staff. 'And I've just heard from DI Murray that the other operation's under way and we should have positive news at any minute. I thought we should be here. I've asked Piper and Miss Bowden to join us.' He was hoping the new American star of the Little Theatre Company wouldn't have time to change back into the Cinderella of Miss Bowden. As Kendrick realised how inappropriately strong his hope was the old annoyance surged, bringing to an end the few euphoric moments he began at once to look back on with nostalgia.

'Have you seen Carol Swain, sir?'

'No. There's time for that. I'm informed there's no fight in her. That she actually seems glad to have been taken into custody.' Kendrick had been strongly tempted to join the team in the next room to Mrs Sheridan, but had held off because he had suspected himself of being influenced by his knowledge that his presence there would ensure him a sight of the American.

'The old *crime passionnel*,' Ted said musingly, and the Chief Superintendent came to attention, recognising one of his

DS's infrequent but regular incursions into his eccentric inner store of philosophies which were usually worth hearing. 'I often think we'd still have capital punishment for cold-blooded murders of strangers if we'd had the sense the French had and not muddled that sort of murder with murders done where people are pushed to the utmost by their deepest emotions.'

'Go on, Ted.' When things were moving smoothly to their conclusion, one could afford to take a little time out.

'No wonder we didn't hang anyone else after we hanged Ruth Ellis. I wonder we hanged anyone after we hanged Edith Thompson. All right, the girl did very wrong, she urged her husband on to kill her lover, but she never raised a finger of her own to anyone, she just wanted that lover all to herself and didn't have any other comfort from education or the classics... When the time came she was almost dead from fear. They had to drag her to the gallows, you know, sir.'

'I had heard. And I think there's a lot in what you've just said.' He did, and he would think about it sometime when the immediate future was less rosy. 'Now, though–'

There was another knock at the door, and

when Kendrick called 'Come!' a uniformed constable put his head round. 'A Dr Piper and a Miss Bowden for you, sir.'

'Show them in, constable.'

The words 'Miss Bowden' had caused a disproportionate fall in the Chief Superintendent's continuing high spirits, but they were immediately uplifted by the sight of the tall slender figure preceding Dr Piper into his office. Not precisely the lady of his grudgingly fond memory, but from the same luxury stable.

'Please come in!' Kendrick found he had gone round his desk to greet them, and was relieved that Ted had brought a chair forward for Miss Bowden before he had time further to abase himself. 'Sit down,' he said, retreating to his own chair, from whence with impeccable legitimacy he smiled on Piper's sidekick as he congratulated her.

'That was very well done, Miss Bowden. We are greatly in your debt.' The annoyance resurging, Kendrick wondered if he would have been able to put it so fulsomely if he had been looking at the severe female to whom the name 'Miss Bowden' had hitherto been attached. 'And you were very brave.'

'I was very well protected, Chief Superintendent.'

'That doesn't detract from your courage.' The annoyance continued as Kendrick realised the extent of his pleasure that it was not Miss Bowden's usual flat tones issuing from the sophisticated beauty in front of him, but the appropriate American huskiness he so vividly remembered.

'Thank you. It will all be in the transcript, of course, but I can't overemphasise how much Carol regrets what she did. I hope she can find a good defence counsel.'

'Her trial will be a *cause célèbre*. There'll be the best of everything all round.'

'That's good. Chief Superintendent–' Miss Bowden leaned towards his desk, and Kendrick decided that although the hair was different the scent was the same. 'I hope the fact that the murders have turned out not to have any connection with drug dealing means that you cleared that up so far as the Little Theatre's concerned with the arrests you've already made.'

'No. But it will be cleared up. Very soon.' Kendrick looked invitingly towards his telephone, and to his gratification it rang. But coincidences happened all the time in real life, he reflected as he picked it up, while, a writer of fiction would have to fall over backwards to avoid them.

'Yes? Ah. Very good. You're bringing them in now? Fine, I'll receive them in person.'

Kendrick got to his feet and stood half turned towards the wide window behind his chair. It had a fine view over the sea, but it was immediately above Reception and also provided a sight of the forecourt where arriving cars drew up.

'We mustn't keep you.'

His visitors were on their feet, but with a smile Kendrick waved them down. 'Don't go just yet. There's something I'd like you to see if you can spare me a little more time.'

'Surely.' Peter and Phyllida exchanged questioning glances, and grew steadily more curious as it became apparent that the Chief Superintendent had no more business to transact with them. To their increasing surprise, his official persona appeared to have been subsumed by a social self, as he asked Miss Bowden in friendly fashion about her impressions of the Little Theatre Company, and the extent of its talents.

But he remained standing at the window, and looking out of it more often than he looked towards his two visitors, and after about ten minutes he stiffened, then beckoned them over.

'Come and have a look, both of you. This should be of particular interest to you, Miss Bowden.'

At first Phyllida couldn't think what they were being asked to look at: all she could see was a police car drawing up and four men getting out of it. Two detectives, by the confidence of their body language. And two prisoners, by the submissiveness of theirs, and the tumbled look of their clothes. One had a bald crown to his head that shone in the light streaming out of the station entrance. The other had a good head of dark hair and...

'Dear God,' Phyllida said aloud, realising why the Chief Superintendent, for the first time in their bizarre relationship, had been able to appear ungrudging in his thanks to the Peter Piper Agency. He had had an ace up his sleeve. He had known he would have the last laugh.

'DS Jones came up trumps, too,' Kendrick said. 'As you can see.'

Peter asked what it was all about.

'It's about Kevin Keithley,' Phyllida told him. 'And one of the stage staff from the Little Theatre. I recognise him but I can't remember his name.' She turned to Kendrick as the men disappeared into the station building. 'Drugs?' she asked.

The Chief Superintendent turned away from the window, nodding. 'Yep. Some instinct told me we'd only scotched the dealing problem inside the theatre company, and the murders of course seemed to bear my instinct out. They could have distracted us, but DS Jones stuck to her brief–' there were times, Kendrick admitted to himself in that moment, when a blinkered vision could be an advantage – 'and came up with the goods in one direction while Miss Bowden came up with them in the other. A good night's work.' Kendrick hesitated. 'I've decided to impose a media blackout on Carol Swain's full motive. It'll be given out that she killed Carson because he was breaking off their engagement. There'll be no mention of the homosexual angle, so you can reassure your client, Dr Piper, that his son's involvement won't come out.'

'Thank you!' Peter and Phyllida responded in fervent chorus.

'Don't be too grateful. It suits my book too.'

The Chief Superintendent hesitated for a second time, but the next moment he had sat down, plunged his hand out of sight beside his desk, and was bringing a bottle of Scotch and three glasses out of a set-up like Peter's. 'A celebratory drink is called for, I think.'

But he wasn't going to ask DS Jones to join them.

'So that must be why Kevin Keithley was so disappointed Mrs Sheridan was leaving,' Phyllida said to Peter the next morning. 'He'd been psyching himself up to try his hand at involving her. The irresistible lure of living at the Golden Lion, as you suggested at the beginning. I suppose I'd better be the one to tell Jenny.'

'I think it would come best from you,' Peter said, firmly but not quite meeting her eyes. It was the sort of task, Phyllida had learned from experience, that he would shun above all others. 'And quickly, I'd say. Quite apart from her starting to wonder where on earth the man is, it'll be on the local news by lunch-time.'

'Yes. I'd like to take her out to do it, but that would put her through too much anxious speculation on the way to wherever we'd go. So it had better be the rest room.'

'Right. I'll keep Steve out if he comes back

314

while you're shut up in there together. And ask Jenny to switch the phone through.'

Phyllida went straight out to Reception and told Jenny there was something she wanted to say to her.

'There's something I want to say to *you*.' Jenny had blushed, and was looking uncomfortable.

'Fine. Let's go into the rest room. Peter's promised to keep Steve out.'

When they were settled in the two armchairs, after a great deal of wriggling about on Jenny's part that didn't appear to succeed in making her comfortable, Phyllida suggested Jenny should speak first.

'No! I mean... What you have to say must be more important, with Peter being in on it.' There was sudden alarm in the big blue eyes. 'It isn't... Oh, God. I haven't seen Mum since last weekend...' Jenny had recently moved into a flat of her own in Seaminster.

'No! No, Jenny, it's nothing to do with your family. But it *is* serious, and it *is* to do with someone important to you. Now, you must be strong. It's about Kevin.'

Phyllida had expected the alarm to come back with the sound of her beloved's name, but to her surprise Jenny's reaction appeared to be embarrassment. 'Look, Jenny,' she went on quickly. 'You know that both Peter and the Chief Superintendent were first interested in the Little Theatre Company because of the drugs connection. Mr Kendrick didn't feel the arrests had taken care of it all, and while we were investigating on behalf of Paul Harper's father, he was carrying on looking for further evidence of drug dealing.' Phyllida paused to gather her forces to administer the pill that could take no sweetening. 'He found two further dealers within the Company, and they were arrested last night. One's one of the stage staff, and the other's Kevin Keithley.'

The eyes she was holding became even wider from astonishment. Phyllida waited unhappily for it to turn into horror, then angry disbelief. But to her own surprise it reverted to embarrassment.

'Jenny? You know what I've just said. Your friend Kevin is a drug dealer.'

'Yes, I heard you. Phyllida... I've been wanting to tell you, but I just couldn't seem to find the opportunity. Me and Kevin, we're not an item any more. I don't know ... I suddenly started to find him boring. He was just as kind, he was still around as much of the time as he's always been, but I began to feel… It sounds stupid, I know, but I began to feel he wasn't really there at all, nobody was there. It got like being out with a cardboard cut-out. Does that make any kind of sense?'

'As things have turned out, maybe it does. Oh, dear.' But she shouldn't be feeling deflated, she should be feeling glad for Jenny's sake, that she couldn't be hurt. 'Well, that's good news, Jenny. Now, I'm sure I know the answer before I ask the question, but can you assure me that Kevin never gave you any information about what he was doing?'

'He never gave me any information,' Jenny repeated solemnly. 'Gosh, what a surprise! No wonder he didn't seem to be there half the time. Now I think of it, he did tend to say he had to do things that seemed a bit odd. Like taking a great-aunt to the dentist.'

'That is odd, yes. Jenny, I'm so glad you're not feeling involved. How long since–'

'Oh, last week. I've got my eye on someone else now.' Jenny blushed again, then gave Phyllida a reassuring smile. 'You can tell Peter it's all right.'

Phyllida saw her own sense of anti-climax mirrored in Peter's reaction, and they both started laughing.

'Thanks to Kendrick I'll be able to spare

Harper senior a final harrowing report,' Peter said, when they had recovered. 'But when he points out – as I'm afraid he will – that although I've given him good news about his son *vis-à-vis* the drug scene, and found no evidence of his having broken the law in any other way, I haven't found out what's wrong with him, I think I'll just have to tell him to refer to the boy himself.'

'Implying that you know what the boy could say, even if he chooses not to?'

'I'll try to keep that ambiguous. Pity I can't ask you to do it,' Peter added wistfully. 'I've got a potential new client coming in in the morning, by the way. Sounds straightforward. I thought I'd give her to you.'

'Thanks.'

'Ten o'clock, please, Miss Bowden. Now, I suggest you take the rest of today off. Out of respect for the passing of Mrs Sheridan, if you like. She was a brave woman. Thanks, Phyllida.'

'I enjoyed it.' And must now confront and rout the sense of bleakness that had overtaken her at the prospect of a day without a brief. The sort of day she had once relished.

'And for goodness' sake book yourself a holiday before things hot up again. You went straight to London and came straight back

318

here without a break.'

'Thanks. I'll think about it.'

She *would* rout the bleakness, Phyllida vowed, as she turned the car on to the Parade. Recover her self-sufficiency. The day was pastel, with a diffused sun turning the sea a myriad delicate colours, and she would take her paints to the bay at Billing, or perhaps farther afield.

That was, after she had done the other thing Peter had suggested: booked herself a holiday.

In Edinburgh.

This Large Print Book for the partially sighted, who cannot read normal print, is published under the auspices of

# THE ULVERSCROFT FOUNDATION